UNDER A
NEON SUN

UNDER A NEON SUN

A NOVEL

KATE GALE

THREE ROOMS PRESS
New York, NY

ISBN 978-1-953103-49-9 (trade paperback)
ISBN 978-1-953103-50-5 (Epub)
Library of Congress Control Number: 2023949906

TRP-113

First edition
Publication Date: April 23, 2024

BISAC Coding:
FIC044000 FICTION / Women
FIC076000 FICTION / Feminist
FIC019000 FICTION / Literary
FIC069000 FICTION / City Life

COVER DESIGN:
KG Design International: www.katgeorges.com

BOOK DESIGN:
KG Design International: www.katgeorges.com

DISTRIBUTED IN THE U.S. AND INTERNATIONALLY BY:
Publishers Group West: www.pgw.com

Three Rooms Press | New York, NY
www.threeroomspress.com | info@threeroomspress.com

For Mark, Tobi, and Stephen—
always

"The sun is a joke.
Oranges can't titillate their jaded palates.
Nothing can ever be violent enough to make
taut their slack minds and bodies."

—Nathanael West, THE DAY OF THE LOCUST

UNDER A NEON SUN

CHAPTER 1

FEBRUARY 10TH, 2020

WHEN I WAKE, I DON'T KNOW where my bra is. It's important to have a bra. If you don't have one, and you go to a job interview, and they see your tits, they'll think you want to fuck them and that's sending the wrong message. Since I'm at the bottom of the American barrel, sending messages of any kind to employers other than, "Please give me a job before I die," is unwise. I live in my car, and I only have one bra. It has to be around here somewhere. I don't like to sleep with the bra on. It's a little scratchy. For those of you who have never worn a bra, let me be honest, you aren't missing much. It's a little stretchy thing that goes around your body and says to your breasts, "Wake up, look straight ahead and look perky." I find my bra under the passenger seat. Very strange. I must have been having weird dreams. I remember one dream. I had a map of America, and the whole thing was on fire. Then I doused it with milk, and it was wet and crumbling. A crumbling America in my fingers. I keep a map of the United States in my glove box in case I ever get the chance to drive across it. I'd like to see its corn and grain, its trees and rivers, the other shining ocean, on the way, maybe some mountains, trees and lakes. What a thing it would be to see the Mississippi. On top of America, floating above it are all the people who went to expensive schools and make a lot of money. I work for those people, and they think they worked hard and deserve everything they have. "Smile," they tell me, and I do. "Smile, and people will like you, and give you what you need." Well, it's a whole lot easier to smile and look beautiful when you went to a good college, live in a fancy house, and have sheets to sleep on at night. Sheets must be nice.

I pull on my flip flops. I step out into the cool morning light threaded down through the trees, and I grab my tissues from the glove box and head for the trees to pee. When I get back, I open the back of my car. The back opens up and stays open and I slip into my sleeping bag so I can enjoy waking. The great thing about a hatchback car is that you can sit in the car and have it open and look out at everything. I sit up and stretch out my legs and feet. I see mostly trees. I pick up a journal and write a few pages. This is the best part of my day. I am alone, no one wants anything from me. Everything I own is in sight. I wish for the millionth time for a dog or a cat, but when you're living out of your car, it's just not fair. I see other homeless people, tent people, with dogs, but I can't see myself doing it. I have a car and a job which means the dog or cat would be left in the car and it would die. The only way it works to be homeless and own a pet is not to work at all, and my plan is to get out of my situation. I am saving money. I am going to get out. Once I've started to wake up, I turn on music. Later in the day, when I'm cleaning houses, I listen to Tom Waits, Lou Reed, Nina Simone, PJ Harvey, but in the morning, I can't bear words. I listen to jazz and classical music, Monk and Mozart. Listening to classical music in my car feels like I'm in a little symphonic space. Once, I'm listening to my work music, I'm in a marching mode.

I chose this parking spot well. The woman who owns this Topanga property is aware that I am parking here, but she does not mind. I stopped at the woman's house and explained my situation as briefly as possible. Normies don't want to hear it. I keep it short. That's what the other homeless people always remind me. This woman's property is the first consistently safe parking space I have found for months. No police rapping on my window. No other homeless people asking for stuff. No men trying to break into my car when they see a woman sleeping alone. The woman seems comfortable with someone living in a car on her property. I'd been told by someone at the market that she is the goddess of the mountain, but she said I could call her Diana.

"As long as you respect the land, young lady," Diana said. Her house was full of crystals, and it had a fire pit in the middle and a bunch of benches around it with blankets. I assumed she either had a lot of parties or it was for some kind of ceremony. She seemed like the ceremony type.

"I'll pick up everything," I said, "leave no trace, I got it."

"I have a wolf," the woman said. She had a lot of wild gray hair and the most piercing blue eyes like someone who could be either twenty or one hundred and twenty. I felt sure that if

I left a speck of trash on her property, she would immediately know about it. "I keep track of my wolf," she says. "He doesn't chase the deer. Don't you disturb the deer either."

"Of course, you have a fucking wolf," I thought. The wolf slipped up quietly behind the woman. "I'll be perfect," I said, "You won't even know I'm here. The deer won't know I'm here either." The woman nodded and I drove down the mountain in my Nissan to find a little out of the way parking spot. After that, she and I would pass each other and wave, but we rarely spoke. She did have ceremonial parties at her house on weekends, and sometimes she paid me to go get supplies for these events, mostly weed, but mostly, I kept to myself. I haven't seen any deer, but I take her word for it. I suppose if you live on the top of a mountain where there are deer, having a wolf would make those deer uncomfortable. When I drive up to drop off the groceries, the place smells like sage and the wind chimes are going. "I'm calling the spirits," she tells me.

I HAVE TO GET MOVING. TUESDAYS and Thursdays I go to Pierce College, but every day I work, and today is my day to clean houses with Sophia. I get up, roll up my sleeping bag next to my small, neat bookshelf, brush my teeth, wash my face, comb my hair, and slide into jeans and a T-shirt. At the bottom of the hill, I am ready to treat Sophia to Starbucks. Sophia would never buy Starbucks for herself, but she loves it when I buy it for her. She's so funny. She loves licking the whipped cream. I always offer to buy it for her so she can have it at her house, and once a year, we get it for her birthday and have it on ice cream, but she says it's silly to buy it all the time.

I have thought many times as I go over my budget that Starbucks is a ridiculous expense in a budget that involves saving every penny toward tuition at UCLA, but Sophia is the only one who has my back, and I know that this coffee is like grace between us and if you are so poor that you lose grace, you've lost everything. I want to keep us even. I clean a couple houses with Sophia, but most of my work is child-care, and I've figured out if I save enough money, I won't have to go into debt for college. I can't graduate and have thousands of dollars to pay off, I don't want to live like that. I can't picture getting a job that will let me pay off college debt. I've asked people about it and they talk about debt that you don't pay off as long as you live. I don't want a life like that. A house debt sure, but a house has equity our economics teacher says. To be honest, I can't picture owning a house, but taking on debt for a house makes sense to me. Student loan debt is the millstone that sinks a generation.

Sophia arrives in a good mood. "Olivia, she is getting such good grades," she says as soon as she sits down. "She is going to do great things, maybe run a store, maybe start a company. She is going to be a true American. She is going to UCLA, just like you." Sophia's daughter, Olivia introduced us when Sophia's sister and cleaning partner moved back to El Salvador. Sophia needed help and Olivia already had a good part-time job at the Pierce College Swimming Pool. We drink our coffee and watch the odd combination of suited people, students, and homeless people sifting in and out of Starbucks. "I brought you lunch," Sophia says, "Some tamales. You're way too thin."

"I am trying to be fashionable; don't mess with me," I say. "How am I going to make it as a model in this town if you keep feeding me tamales?" She laughs. She knows how much I love her tamales.

"Mia, I'm watching you" she says, "let's go."

We arrive at the first job and swing into action. The couple we are cleaning for is retired. They like to golf and garden, and the old guy has a man cave where he spends most of his time. When we go to clean there, we've been instructed to knock on the door. "What do you think he's doing in there?" Sophia whispers.

"Watching porn," I reply. "Come on, Mama." In moments of closeness, I call her "Mama."

"But he's so old."

"That doesn't stop men. Nothing stops them. They're always at it. Filthy beasts."

"Why do you talk like that? You need a boyfriend? If you had a boyfriend, you could live with him in his apartment, take showers every day. It's ridiculous how you live. You're like one of those gringas under the bridge."

"You're not going to see me under the bridge. I keep my car running. I have a savings account for my car."

"You don't keep your money in your car, do you?"

"I must look like a gringa idiot. No, I do not. I keep it in the bank. Like a person. Where do you keep your money, under the mattress?"

"You know Roberto does not trust American banks. We keep it hidden at the apartment."

"What if your apartment gets robbed?"

"It's a really good hiding place."

"What are you saving for?

"Rainy day. But things are good in America. I don't know if there will be any rainy days. It doesn't rain in California. Why have a rainy-day fund? I want to have a new dress. I keep getting new jobs. Most jobs I can do by myself, but I'll let you know if I need help on any other jobs. I could do this one alone, but they were used to two people getting in and out in three hours, so it's nice, we can do two jobs in a day. And it's more fun."

The woman comes along behind us and has us come back and clean tiny bits of dust we leave behind. She stops watching television after each room is completed to examine it carefully for any sign that we have not done an immaculate job. We wash the clothes and hand wash her bras and underwear, we clean up cat litter tracked around the kitchen, change the litter box, and bring in new cat food and litter. We take away the recyclables which we split between us at each house that we clean. At the end of the cleaning day, the woman often gives clothing or household goods to Sophia, stuff she is giving to Goodwill. The woman gives each of us fifty dollars, and we go on to our next job.

Our next job is a much bigger house. It is in Calabasas and the family is having a pool party. We set to work, cleaning the kitchen, the dishes, the laundry. We can usually get through this house in four hours if we really hit it, but only because we clean this house every week. We can hear shouts of laughter from the pool, and at some point, a boy from the party wanders into the kitchen. "Get me a beer," he says, as if

I were his own personal bartender. When we started this job, we were told that we were never allowed to open the fridge. If the fridge needed to be cleaned, the woman would have everything on the counter when we arrived and we would clean it and put everything back in. "Previous house cleaners thought it was okay to snack from my fridge, so I now have a strict no fridge rule and of course, the no snacking rule goes to the rest of the house. You need to bring your own snacks. If you need water, there's the spigot."

"I can't open the fridge," I said. "I'm not allowed." I can see Sophia, who is putting away dish towels, watching me. The lady of the house is under an umbrella by the pool wearing dark sunglasses.

"She can't open the fridge," the boy says, "you can." Sophia stops suddenly what she is doing and cocks her head like she is waiting for a response from me. I think of all the things I could say, like, *"Get your own frickin' beer,"* but then we both might be out of a job and where would that take us? I open the fridge, take out a beer, open the drawer, snap the top for him, and hand him the bottle. "That wasn't so hard," he says. He is wearing board shorts and no shirt. I imagined he and his sister, and all his friends, go to private school and to private colleges and call their parents, "Okay boomer," and think they know everything. "What do you do besides this?" He waves his hand.

"I go to Pierce," I say.

"Well, isn't that fun? Taking a few night classes? Trying to get ahead? Good for you. Make a little life yourself; you should get a boyfriend. One of those Pierce College boys."

His hand runs down my back to my buttocks and I don't make a sound. "See you around," he says.

"What was that?" Sophia says as soon as we were upstairs. "What the heck?"

"It happens," I say. "Let's stay together. We're almost done." This job is one hundred for each of us and we both need it. I am not going to screw it up.

When the woman pays us, she asks if I will house sit for the weekend. House sitting—my ideal job. I shower every day, eat normal food, swim in the pool, and pretend to be a normal person. "Sure," I say, "when do you need me to be here?"

"Can you get here Thursday night? We're driving to Santa Barbara, but I'd like to get out of here Thursday. It's for Valentine's Day, but the kids are staying with friends."

"Sure," I say, "should I bring my own food?"

"No," she says, "help yourself. I'll be here with the key, and I'll go over the instructions. Five p.m.? We can give you a hundred dollars a day."

"Sure," I say. I would have done it for half that, but this is Calabasas. Sophia and I usually talk for a few minutes as we leave jobs. She's on her way home to make dinner for her family, and I'm on my way to Pierce to swim at the pool and get a shower. I call and she picks up right away.

"You coming to dinner Saturday?" she asks.

"Would I miss it?"

"Just making sure you don't have a hot date."

"Sure, with that guy back at the house. I'm going to be waiting on him while I live my little life."

"You can't blame them," she says. "We're little people to them. Everyone who doesn't have money, we're just little people." She laughs. Every Saturday I go to Sophia's apartment, and I bring beer and oranges. They've offered for me to stay with them, but there are three people in that one-bedroom apartment, and I can't do that to them. I would be paying rent and that would make it impossible for me to save for UCLA.

"I'm worried about this virus," she says.

"That thing is halfway around the world. I don't think it's making it to California."

"You need to listen to the news. It's already here. It's probably been here for months. They found cases in San Diego. I think it's here; I think it's everywhere."

"What do you think will happen?"

"I don't know. I am thinking twice now about what I said earlier about the rainy day. Something might be coming toward us that we don't have any idea about."

"Don't scare me. I just got a really good gig. I'll see you this weekend. Dos Equis?"

"You know it. Don't worry, maybe it's nothing. Maybe it will just go away. Roberto says immigrants worry too much. Always see problems coming over the horizon. We should see sunshine. See you Saturday."

CHAPTER 2

FEBRUARY 25TH

"RICHARD AND I HAVE GOT TO go away for the weekend or I am going to kill somebody or myself. Not literally. But I have got to get out of here. I never recovered from the holidays. All that entertaining and having the in-laws over and the parties," Sheryl and her friend Candy sit by her pool in the cabana.

"What about the kids?" Candy doesn't have kids, and although she is "Aunt Candy," she never gets saddled with actual childcare.

"Mia is coming in. She'll be here in a few minutes."

"Everyone uses Mia," Candy says.

"Well, she's reliable and the kids love her."

"You just don't think she would steal from you because she's white. I don't think any of the Salvadoran girls ever take anything from you, but you're always watching them."

"Maybe you're right. She feels like one of us. She's a college student. She's going to UCLA. She could be my daughter. To tell the truth, I think of her like another daughter. I give her clothes. I'm always looking out for her. I'd do anything for her. Last week, she had a flat tire and I had Richard go out and help her change it right away. We even gave her a turkey for Thanksgiving."

"Where does she live?"

"Somewhere in the Valley, near Pierce I think. I've never really asked, but I think her parents spoiled her and then she just decided that she wanted to make her own money. I'm proud of her. You can tell she likes to live simply but really has good taste by the way she arranges flowers."

"Where are you going?"

"Bacara, you know I love Bacara."

"Are you packed?"

"I like having Jessica pack for me. She packs for a lot of the women around here. She's so good at it. She packs for our business trips and now I have her pack for everything. She looks to see what our restaurant reservations are, what museums we're going to, I mean in Santa Barbara it doesn't matter, but we are going out on a friend's boat. She picks everything out so perfectly; I can just relax and know it's done. When you go to New York or DC, it's so great, she will have everything picked out for every meeting."

"I prefer to throw a third of my wardrobe in the backseat and hope there's something suitable when I arrive," Candy says. "Are you worried about this pandemic business?"

"No. They'll get it under control. The government people. When have we ever really had a situation where we had a pandemic close down the country? Never. It's mostly China."

"The market is in free fall and Bill Gates says this is a once in a century pandemic."

"I hate Bill Gates and I don't trust him. He might have caused this whole thing himself just to make himself richer."

"Slow down there sister, how much Fox News do you watch?"

"Enough. I just get bored when I'm working on my graphic projects at home and Richard's at the hospital. What Bill wants is to implant a microchip in all of our brains along with a vaccine."

"Okay, let's say Bill Gates is an evil monster. Why would he want to do this? He's rich. He gives money away at an alarming rate. I get that a lot of those Silicon Valley types give money to people in Africa rather than help people in America. No doubt it's sexier to get in your private jet and fly to Africa and help over there than to help out the eight thousand homeless people in San Francisco where those very rich people go to dine and shop. But Bill Gates?"

"Half of Americans hate Bill Gates."

"Actually, half of Fox viewers which isn't the same thing. Americans are paranoid and smoke too much weed."

"You don't watch Fox News?"

"No, and except for you, I don't have any friends that watch Fox News. I try not to be friends with people who watch it. It's garbage. It's for the Silent Generation who I wish would be a little more silent and quit voting. I wasn't aware that you were watching it. It's going to rot your brain. Look, I get hating Microsoft. That's an American pastime. They had a monopoly on the operating system we all used, and they used that to shovel low quality software down our gullets until we choked on it. But saying that he's so creepy that he wants to microchip all Americans is part of the problem here. I get paranoia. I get not believing we landed on the moon. I mean if we landed on the moon, why were all the moon flights when Nixon was president? And why haven't we gotten through the Van Allen belts since Nixon was president? But just starting to believe that Bill Gates who looks like he eats tofu for breakfast wants to microchip Americans is a problem."

"What problem?"

The St. Mary kids burst through the French doors and onto the patio with their father behind them. "When is Mia getting here?" Richard says, "I'm going upstairs to my office. They're all yours now."

"That's her now. Mia, let the kids play games, I want to relax out here, and see if they want food and if they do, order them something." Mia gives the twins a look and they bound toward her and into the house. They have a wing in their bedrooms with a sitting area and a game console. When Sheryl talks, they look at each other and laugh. She doesn't remember when they started ignoring her. If no one is there except the three of them, they start a little comedy routine except it's not funny, where one says, "Is she talking to us?" and the other says, "I don't know. I think her mouth is moving, but I'm pretty sure no words are coming out?" and the other one will say, "Where are the words going?" and then they'll start, "Oh, the words, the little words, they're slipping away," and they'll start slipping and sliding around the room, like her slippery little words keep escaping them and they want to find them and bring them back, but they don't know how, and when they tire of that game, they have endless more. They'll cock their heads and say, "I'm deaf, are you deaf?" and the other will say, "I'm deaf, are you deaf?" There's no end.

Sheryl tries sometimes to remember when this started. She will sit in the corner crying, "You know that I dread being left alone with you boys. You know you guys will be the death of me. I'm your own mother, how can you treat me like this?" That really gets them going.

"Is it crying?" they'll say to each other. "Is it weeping? Is it having little wet stuff come out of its little eyeballs?" She has considered therapy. She has considered telling somebody, but anyone she could tell would be telling someone that her own two sons are monsters, possibly psychopaths. She can't do that. She has to hope they grow out of this, and as far as she can see, she's the only one being treated like this. Maybe, she was too easy on them when they were babies. Maybe she gave them too many toys, breastfed them too long. Gave them too much sugar. She has so many clients. There were rafts of stuffed animals, every toy they could imagine, music lessons, horseback riding, martial arts. They've had it all.

"The problem," Candy says "is that Americans always want someone to blame, someone to hate. Bill Gates is a rich man who got rich shafting Americans, but I don't think that means he wants to microchip us. One doesn't follow the other. Hilary Clinton was married to a philanderer; that doesn't mean she's part of a ring that's selling children as sex slaves. Americans are like five-year-olds. They believe in purple dinosaurs and that Bert and Ernie might be gay."

"You may be right. I don't know. Also, are we sure Bert and Ernie aren't gay?"

"I think it would cool if they were. Such role models."

"Let me go see if Mia and the kids are okay. I'll be back and we can finish this wine."

Sheryl pads into the house in her flip flops and turns on the television. More bad news. "Mia," she yells. She hears Mia talking to the boys and then coming down the hallway. "What do they want?"

"They want Indian food. Shall I order enough for you and Richard as well?"

When did they start ordering out almost every night, she wonders. Wasn't there a time when they used to cook dinners together? She can't remember how long ago that's been. Upstairs, Richard is in his office with the news on. "What's up, honey?"

"Mia's ordering Indian for the twins. What do you want for dinner? Same?"

"Sure, honey, we can eat downstairs. Let her eat with them in their room while they watch TV. We need to talk. Is Candy leaving?"

"Yeah, she's about to take off." She brushes his hair with her hands and goes downstairs. "Candy, I have to get ready for dinner." Candy has already brought in the wine and is gathering her things.

"I'll be in touch," she says, and blows kisses as she walks out the door. "Stop watching Fox News. Read *The New York Times*. I'll send it to you, you can download it on your phone, okay?"

The housekeeper and the gardener have come and gone, the man who vacuums and washes the cars too, so the house is in order and ready for them to leave for the weekend. Sheryl checks her suitcase which is packed and ready for Santa Barbara. They plan to eat dinner one night at Bouchon and one night at the hotel restaurant. They always like Bouchon. They go there by car service so they can drink as much as they like. When the Indian food arrives, Richard and Sheryl sit down in the dining room with their naan, rice, tandoori, and vegetables. They went to India last summer and the food was so different there, but they agree this Indian takeout place is pretty good. Richard is always calm; that's one of the things Sheryl likes about him. The house after the twins arrived felt like the deck of a ship that things were always sliding from one side to the other, but Richard is always a calming presence, always there to bring on more help.

"Honey," he says, "I've been looking into this virus situation, and if it gets worse, if it really becomes a pandemic, they'll tell all of us to shelter at our houses and not to see other people."

"What does that mean?"

"Shelter in place means you would be at your house and people would not come over. Just you and the kids. I would be at the hospital."

Sheryl stops eating. "How soon could this happen?"

"I don't know. But it could. It could happen. We'd be fine. We have food stored up. We have a generator in case the power goes out; you work from home on your projects so you can supervise the boys if they have to do online schoolwork. I'll feel bad for Mia if she loses all her jobs, but I'm sure, she'll go back to her parents or whoever. These Gen Zers are resilient; they all have plenty more money than we did at that age. We will all be fine." Sheryl loves baingan barta, and at that moment had been ready to spoon some on her plate, but she has paused in midair. "Are you okay, honey? Did you drink wine earlier?"

"No," she says, "it was just Candy drinking the wine. Just a moment." She leaves the table. Richard slices himself a piece of lamb tandoori.

"Are you okay in there?" He can hear his wife steadily vomiting in the powder room. He pauses. He hears her swishing the mouthwash and then she comes back to sit at the end of the table. "What's up?" he says, "seriously?"

"I'm having a panic attack."

"Mia's here," Richard says, "we can leave first thing in the morning." He gets up and goes to talk to Mia, leaving Sheryl alone. Sheryl stares at the food. The last time they went to Santa Barbara, they went by train, and it took forever to get home because someone threw themselves in front of the tracks. They had to wait four hours for the body to be cleared. It was a woman; they had been told. She thinks of that woman now. Was she lying face down or face up as the train sped toward her?

CHAPTER 3

―――

MARCH 6TH

I PULL UP TO CHUCK AND Sally's house alongside Sophia's little Tacoma truck. Chuck's Mercedes is in the driveway and beside it there's another car we don't recognize. Sally claims that Chuck doesn't have any friends except her, so this must be one of her friends. We clean this house twice a week, once in the morning, once in the afternoon so they'll have a clean house going into their weekend. Sophia always hits the kitchen first, washing the dishes, taking everything out of the fridge and she's a demon with the oven cleaning. I get the bathrooms, the laundry, and the pantry. We both do the floors and mopping together at the end. It's strange how much easier it is to do a housecleaning job when you have a partner. We don't talk much; she listens to music in Spanish. I listen to Pandora, my Lou Reed, Tom Waits, and Nina Simone; music keeps us going. While we are at the house, the gardeners are there too, so sometimes, Sally has us come out to translate.

Today, we enter the house, to the smell of Thai food and the sound of a party going on in the backyard. "Wait here a minute," I say. "Let me check on everything. Maybe they forgot we were coming today." I step onto the patio and there's Chuck lying naked in the backyard two girls on either side of him. "There's party music playing and one of the girls is in a bikini and doing a dance for him not too sexy like a club dance, but definitely a shake your booty dance. He stands up to say hello, and what goes through my mind right away is, "He's not circumcised."

"Hello, Mia," he says, "this is Gia and her friend. They're just coming to use the pool. Sally is visiting her mother for a few days in Florida, so you run along and get the house clean and let me know when you're finished and then feel free to come out and join us. The more the merrier."

"No problem," I say. And then, because I'm such an idiot, I say, "Is there anything I can get you?" and he says, "Bring out the vodka and the bottle of lime juice on the counter." I bring him the vodka and lime and get back to Sophia. "He's naked in the backyard with two girls."

"Working girls?"

"I don't think so. They looked nice."

"Are you saying hookers are skanky?"

"Well, these girls look like they might be students, or I don't know, they might be even in high school, maybe they just entertain old men on the side. Or maybe they're really his girlfriends."

OFTEN CHUCK AND SALLY HAVE DINNER separately. He makes himself a sandwich and takes it back to his man cave and she makes a salad or opens a can of soup for herself and watches something on television. But once recently when we came over, Sally was making dinner for both of them. "The president's going to be speaking on Fox News," Sally said. "We've started eating dinner together every night and watching Fox News."

"Why would you do that?" I ask.

"What?" she says.

"Why would you ruin your dinner by watching Fox News?"

"He loves the president."

"Wait a minute," I say. "How did you, a leftie political campaign manager end up married to someone who loves this president."

"Good in bed. I had dated all these guys who really sucked in the sack and along comes Chuck, and he was smashing. He had moves. I'm telling you, serious moves. Plus, he was into kink. It turns out Republicans are into kink."

"You know there are Democrats who are good in bed. And fucking everybody's into kink. I mean, maybe not people in Arkansas, I don't know. I've never been there. Anyway, that's a reason to have an affair. Not a reason for a thirty-year marriage."

"We have stuff in common. We go out to theater and the Philharmonic, and most of the time I'm with my girlfriends, and I'm trying to see his side of it and watching Fox News is a way of doing that."

"I couldn't do it."

"He's a good man. He doesn't cheat on me. He doesn't hit me."

"Oh stop."

"Stop what?"

"You realize you sound like you're a hundred years old. That's like bragging that your house sitter doesn't steal from you. That's kind of a bare minimum you know, the no cheating and no hitting."

"Gen Zers want too much out of marriage. You want partnership, friendship, equality. You want conversations. Good luck with that." She arranges her dishes in perfect order. "Men don't know how to listen. They don't know how to have conversations. They just look at you, reach for you, talk at you. Their words just flow over you. And here's the thing, marriage isn't a partnership. It's a long slog of two people living side by side in the same house living similar lives and managing not to kill each other. Every morning you wake up and you say, to yourself, I don't want to fucking go to jail for killing him, and you make it through another day, and some days are really okay. Sort of like eating oatmeal cereal."

"Looking forward to that. I can't wait. Oatmeal cereal. I guess I was hoping for a life of picnics, champagne, and I don't know, at least fish tacos. But oatmeal cereal it is. I don't get it though, what keeps you going?"

"Well not my husband, it's all the stuff that happens outside my house, my girlfriends, lunches, traveling to see my family. During the time I'm around my husband which isn't that much, I can make it work." I think about that conversation with Sally as I look out the window at Chuck chatting with the two girls by the pool.

WHEN SOPHIA AND I FINISH UP, I go outside to where Chuck is wrapped in a towel to see if I can collect our money.

"Come sit down," he says. "Beautiful girl, we never get any time together. Sally always has you racing all around the house doing stuff. Come sit."

Oh my god, I think. *This is bad.* But I'm used to doing what adults tell me to do. I sit down.

"Look," he says, "don't judge me too harshly, I met Gia and her friend at the nail shop where I go and get pedicures."

"Do men get pedicures?"

"I do. I love having a woman attend to my feet and legs. It reminds me of Vietnam. Even though Gia is actually from Thailand."

Gia looks at me steadily and I suspect she hasn't had much to drink. Has she been pouring her vodka on the lawn? "We are Chuck's American girlfriends," she says. "Chuck gets us fancy handbags." She picks up two handbags to show me. "And he buys us such yummy Thai food, reminds us of home. Chuck is very nice to us. He's going to buy us diamonds."

"Being at that nail shop reminds me of Vietnam. When I was in Vietnam, I lived with two thirteen-year-old girls."

"Did you now?" I say although I've heard this story many times before. Whenever I'm cleaning his man cave, he talks to me and the subject of these two thirteen-year-old girls who he apparently found somewhere and then brought to live with him as concubines for a year. It's one of his favorite Vietnam memories.

"I saved them." I've always thought that he thinks of himself as having saved the children, but I'm never sure they saw it that way.

"So these two girls remind you of those children?"

"Being in Vietnam was the best time of my life," he says. "That's why I'm so proud of the president. He's getting rid of all these people coming across the border. These people are animals," Sophia steps onto the patio. "All these illegals bringing drugs across the border need to be stopped. They're trash." I am watching Sophia, but we are sober and unpaid, and he is drunk and has our money, so we stay cool. "Why don't you two have dinner with us," he says.

Sophia speaks up then. "I have plans for dinner with my family and Mia's invited because it's Mia's birthday." It isn't my birthday until April, but whatever gets us out of here.

"Get my pants," he says. I go the man cave. In the man cave, the computer is on Pornhub, and hung over the chair are his trousers which I collect. He fishes into his wallet and pays us each one hundred dollars. As soon as he pays us, he drops the towel, and lies down on the chair and the two girls begin to massage his feet and then his legs.

WE CAN HARDLY WAIT FOR OUR usual check in call when we bounce out of there.

Sophia asks, "Do you think they are getting paid?"

"It's hard to say. This can't be fun for them. He's seventy-five. How much Viagra do you think he's taking to keep all this going?"

"How long do you think this has been going on?"

"Quite a while. It's weird to think that many people live their whole life wishing to go back to some other time when they were happy. For many people it was high school. For him, it was Vietnam and it's all been downhill since then. Nothing else with quite the adrenaline rush of the military."

"If the two of them ever have to spend any real time together, I can't imagine what would happen. I mean if they were forced to be in the same house for months or something."

"God forbid. She would be miserable. I think she married him for sex and then stopped liking it."

"You'd think rich people could be happy."

"You'd be wrong."

"What was the best time of your life?" Sophia asks.

"Right now, and I plan to always to say that. Right now is always going to be the best time of my life because I'm going to make it so."

"What went wrong that you ended up living in your car? You've never told me and I didn't want to ask."

"I'll come over early on Saturday and help you cook and I'll tell you."

"What happens if Sally comes home early?"

"None of our business."

"What if she finds out we knew."

"We'll say that he told us to be quiet."

"Right now, the weather is perfect and even when it rains, I'm assuming you find a dry place to park, but what do you do when it's over one hundred?"

"Well, it's a lot less safe because I can't lock my car. At first, I sleep with the windows open but eventually, the whole hatchback is open, and I might as well be sleeping on the ground. That's when I really wish I had a dog. Right now, I'm good because I'm camping on some woman's land. We'll see how long that lasts."

"Why don't you do stuff for her so she'll like keeping you around?"

"I'm trying. I run errands."

"Make it so she can't live without you."

"Got it."

"That's what I do with every single client."

"That's what I do with my childcare clients, but this is a healer and a medicine woman. She has a wolf."

"She's still a person. She needs someone to run to the store and get stuff. Even more so if she lives alone and wants to be talking with the Great Spirit or whatever. You need to be ready to get whatever she needs."

"I'm on it."

I KEEP THINKING ABOUT THE GIRLS, their hands working their way up further to the sound of Destiny's Child "Bootylicious." All I can think is that I hope they don't have inquisitive neighbors, but in Los Angeles, nobody cares what you do. You can have parties and affairs and climb in and out of your own windows and doors all day long and good luck with anyone caring at all. Nobody cares about helping anyone in this city. People watch their neighbors get robbed and smoke another blunt.

CHAPTER 4

MARCH 13TH

I RUN ERRANDS HOUSE FOR AN old man named Ed who lives alone on Mulholland Drive, and today, he's worried about the pandemic and running out of food, so he has me going to Costco. The first time we ever went there, he got me a card in my own name which lives at his house. You can only shop at Costco if you have your own card. But it's funny to me that he thinks that I would sneak and use the Costco card on my own. I pull up in his truck and load up with eight hundred dollars of toilet paper, frozen food, vegetables, rice, beans, eggs, crackers, cheese, more food than he can possibly eat, laundry soap, water, salt, pepper; it's enough to feed an army. When I get back to his house, I put everything on shelves in the spare bedroom. I put all the paper goods together, the canned goods together, and I fill up his extra freezer. He has me check his generator to make sure it's ready for him to turn on, but he says that if he has to turn it on, he's going to call me.

"Why me? Don't you have anyone else?"

"There are steps involved with that thing. I've never done it. So if the electricity goes out, drive right here and I'll give you one hundred dollars to turn the generator on. The instructions are right on it. I don't want to be without power. Aren't Gen Zers supposed to be handy with stuff like this?"

"Oh, we are so handy," I say. "We're nifty."

"Do you have time to come back tomorrow?" he says. "I want you to make another run, I'll pay you another hundred. We're going to fill up the house." The house is six thousand square feet. We end up filling up three of the bedrooms with honey and peanut butter, many rolls of toilet paper and paper towels; he is ready for anything. The old man has five children, but none of them speak to him. I've never really asked, but I asked the housekeeper, and I know the first set live with their mother and the second set used to visit him but eventually they stopped.

Once, when I was there at his house around the holidays I asked if he wanted me to decorate and he said, "For what? The kids don't come around, their mothers turned them against me." Which made me wonder if kids aren't supposed to blame their parents for their relationships after they are thirty, if maybe parents should stop blaming the other parent for their relationship with their kids once the kids turn thirty as well. At that point, your kids are adults, you can reach out to them, build your own relationship with them, but I guess sometimes it's too late. Sometimes the kid has built a wall so thick that you can't get through and you're the demon on the other side. Which of course always makes me think of my own parents. I always tell myself to be ready to forgive anything, but I was not dealt a good hand in the parent department. My father has an excuse for exiting the scene early, but Mother? What was her excuse?

When I work at Ed's house, I always bring myself the same thing for lunch: a can of tuna. It's funny that with all the food he has in his house, it never occurs to him to offer anything to me. I'll say to him, "I'm going to sit down and take a quick break." I say this because he follows me around and directs everything I'm doing.

He takes a break at the same time and has his housekeeper bring him out lunch which is usually a little spread of bagel with smoked salmon, sliced red onions, and capers or sometimes he'll have a caprese salad or a crab salad. I open my can of tuna with my own opener and eat it with my own plastic fork which I rinse afterward. Sometimes before I'm finished my can, he'll say, "Time to get back work. Time's a-wasting, missy."

The housekeeper's job is to keep the house clean, do the laundry, and do the cooking. I am supposed to run him to his doctor appointments and do any other errands that he needs. The housekeeper and I will often work together on projects while he sleeps in the afternoon.

I keep my schedule on my Google calendar, but sometimes at night, I dream that I drive to the wrong house and show up there wearing no shorts, only flip flops. I told a teacher about this dream once, and she laughed and told me she was always dreaming of standing up to teach and realizing she was wearing no pants. The dream of being unprepared. I am not prepared for my life, that's for sure. Parents start kids off with the tools to build their life, and maybe my life is hanging by string because I don't have parents.

I can't imagine what I would do if my own parents wanted to see me again. My mother joined a cult when I was a baby and divorced my father. At the cult, I was not allowed to see my mother or my brother. I was raised with the girls as a trainee to be one of the leader's "girls." We had to do yoga and stay fit, and we were supposed to learn to play musical instruments and sing which I failed at so I was going to be the comedian. Every year, our leader Y, his real name was Jonathan Mansfield but he went by, Y would be given a new group of concubines because he believed himself to be the new David, loved by God. We always had to read the story of David and the story of Solomon. Jonathan had a lot of wives and concubines as did Solomon, and we were ready to join the ranks. I was pretty sure being funny was going to get me further with Y than sitting in the corner playing a guitar or singing a song. My brother was an amazing singer, and I used to hear him singing for Y when he was young. Y would have him as the entertainment around the campfire, and a couple times I ran into him, and we talked a little. I suggested we run away, but he wouldn't talk about it. He disappeared when I was eleven. He was just at the age that he was going to join the orgies, and most of the boys were fainting with joy. I thought at the time, that maybe he was a gentleman, and didn't want to get into screwing all the girls? He seemed aloof. The boys his age were already taking girls as they pleased, but not my brother. A real gentleman, I thought. I missed the sound of his voice, very high and clear.

When I was fourteen, I was presented to Y. The ceremony was supposed to be one year later. But the idea was to get Y excited about the next crop coming up. There were five of us, and I was supposed to be the chatty one. Until I was in the presence of Y. He had a big beard. I hate beards. He had thick eyebrows. I've looked up to see how old he is, and Y is forty-five, but I thought he was ancient. He felt over my whole body starting with my ankles and working his way up. When he was finished, I was ready to vomit. Up until that time, I was excited to meet Y, ready for whatever was next, I don't know what I thought was going to happen. They hadn't told us. But then I knew. I knew in my body what was going to happen to me, and I knew the only way to avoid it was to leave.

I waited until a night when the adults were drinking and that's when I made a run for it. I had taken trips into Santa Cruz, so I knew which way to go, and I hitchhiked into town and then kept going. As far as I know, my mother never tried to get me back. She had a brother James, and I had his number, but I never called. Somehow an unknown uncle didn't seem any more helpful than my unknown father. I've looked up the Church of Y, and they're still there in the Santa Cruz mountains worshipping the sun and following the directions of Y.

What I found out during the months that followed is that a lot of people who are unsheltered in California are teenagers. When I did the research, they say, two hundred thousand teenagers are drifting in California and maybe a third of us are LGBT. When I meet youth with unstable housing, it always feels like half of us are queer, so many kids turned out of homes because their parents weren't cool with them being gay. Those kids took me in while I was in San Francisco and helped me find work, but they suggested moving down here because it's cheaper. It was going to be hard to stay in the Bay and not do anything illegal with my lack of skills. But if I wanted to go to college, I needed to know what city I was born in, so I could get my birth certificate, and that's when I got in touch with my father. I tracked him down and gave him a call. Turns out, he's now a banker with Goldman Sachs. He told me I was born in San Francisco and good luck. That was all. If I had been my brother, it would have been different, I knew that. But my brother had already disappeared into the netherworld. Was already gone.

I camped outside San Francisco for a short while, but then I decided LA would be better and hitchhiked down here. As soon as I arrived, the trucker who had given me a ride stopped at Whole Foods, so I wandered in. The place seemed overwhelming. I walked around trying to register where I was. All this produce stacked up. I ran into this woman by accident, but she also was not looking, and we both apologized. She asked me what I did. I said I was a college student and a nanny and house sitter. She gave me a job on the spot house sitting for the summer. Their house had cameras and she had someone who checked on me, so I guess she felt safe with me. She said she could read my aura. She paid me two thousand for the summer and I used it to buy a little hatchback Nissan. I registered as an orphan and started Pierce College. In San Francisco, I spent weeks looking for my brother. I figured that was the first city he would go to, but no sign of him.

Until I got here. He's here. In Los Angeles. He lives on the streets; I have a friend who keeps an eye on him. Sooner or later, he'll be ready for rehab, and I've got free rehab on speed dial. Until then, Tony helps me keep track of him. I count on Tony.

When I'm ready to finish for the day at the old man's house, the housekeeper comes out to talk with me. "My mom is sick in El Salvador," she says. "I might need to go back home for a few days. I don't think I'll get stuck there. I have a green card, but just in case, I'm leaving all the instructions in case you have to come in and help him out."

"I've never been alone with him. I don't know how to do all that stuff you do."

"His meals are very simple. I'll leave enough stuff in the fridge for the next few days. I'm flying tomorrow, hopefully this will be a short trip. One more thing though."

"What? You look serious."

"He's never really done anything, but he is a bit handsy. I think he has his eye on you. I'd watch myself. Just be careful. I mean he's old, what could he do?"

"Right," I say. "Probably not much."

CHAPTER 5

MARCH 19TH

SHERYL CALLS ME, "WHAT DOES SHELTER at home really mean. I mean, my husband says I need to stay home, but seriously?"

"It means if you are not an essential worker, you can't leave your house. No restaurants. No going to the office. He will still be going to the hospital, but you will need to do your meetings by Zoom."

"Can we still have the gardener?"

"The gardener is outside, so sure, but nobody in the house."

"Wait, does this mean I'm not getting my hair done or my nails done, and what about facials? And let's be clear, I need Ivy to come out and do my IV. I get headaches."

"I'm not the boss of you, but they are saying no physical contact. All hair salons and nail salons are closed, but this isn't going to be for very long. You look great."

"So, my husband's life is going to be the same and my life is being upheaved. I am going to kill myself while he is doing just dandy. Is that just about it? Men are going to be fine.

Women are going to have to clean, do laundry, and do all kinds of shit they haven't done in forever? He is going to be perfect. My fucking life is over. And I am going to have Ivy come when I have a migraine and hook me up to an IV. I kiss the ground she walks on. I could marry her."

"Right, well, you want to call me when this lets up?"

"My husband thinks he is going to have to stay at a hotel by the hospital. I need Ivy. I need Botox. I need to get my nails done. I need weed. Mia, I can't take this. I am going to call you for help."

"You have my number."

"I was wondering if you could still video chat with the boys. They're going to miss you. Just when you're at your parents' house or at the gym or wherever."

"I won't be at the gym," I say. "Gyms are closed."

"Oh yeah, I forgot. Well, can you video chat with them anyway. They would really like it. They're going to miss you. You know I love you like a daughter. And I'll have you come back as soon as we can."

"I don't know," I say. "I'll have to see. You be safe. Let me know if anything changes."

When I get off the phone, I take out a pen and paper and start doing the math. Of the jobs I had before this happened, I still have the job with the Ed which I'm going by this afternoon to run one more errand and I haven't heard from Chuck and Sally, so I'm guessing that's still in play. Everyone else has called to cancel me and say, "Good luck with school and I hope you can go stay with your parents for a while until this thing blows over." That means

I've gone from making two thousand a month to making maybe four hundred a month. At two thousand a month, I can save between ten to fifteen thousand a year toward UCLA depending on car problems. Sadly, two thousand a month is not enough for me to go to a community college and have my own apartment. I would have to come up with first and last month's rent and monthly rent plus utilities. It's better this way. I don't eat much, and I buy my books used. But now, I'm down to making almost nothing. I have the semester to finish out and I have no library to go to, no laptop, just my phone which is not going to work to write papers. If I had a Chromebook, I could probably write the papers in the parking lot of a Starbucks, but I don't have one.

I drive to Ed's house. He wants me to make a Trader Joe's run and I take his list and get him smoked salmon, plums, hummus, goat cheese, basil, fresh squeezed orange juice, tortillas, and salsa. There is a long line at Trader Joe's. When I'm finished putting the things away, I go find him to get paid. He's listening to Bach in the living room. He's left the money on the table. I pick it up and his hand covers mine. I don't move. I turn and look him in the eyes. "We have an understanding," I say. "Juanita is in El Salvador and you might need me to fill in. I'm happy to help out. I need to know that I'm safe. Am I safe, Mr. Michaelsen?"

"My name's Ed," he says.

"Ed, am I safe?" I say. I'm not fourteen. I don't plan to run away. I want this job and I think I can handle this.

"You're safe," he says, "I just want . . . "

"If you want anything besides what you're paying me to do, you can get a girlfriend or call a hooker. I am not either. Are we clear?"

"Can you make me a martini before you leave? I'll toss you another twenty," he says.

"Sure thing," I say. "Gin or vodka."

"Grey Goose, dry, extra olives," he says.

I walk into the kitchen, lay my phone on the counter and google "vodka martini." When I bring him the finished drink, he raises it to his lips. "Nicely done," he says and opens his billfold. There's a large stack of twenties and he peels one off for me. "Will you be back tomorrow?" he asks. "I'll need an omelet for breakfast."

CHAPTER 6

___

MARCH 20TH

"TELL ME ABOUT YOUR PARENTS," ED says the next morning while I lay out his omelet, berries, and coffee. "I get the feeling if you could be living with them you would be and you aren't."

"My mother's in a cult," I say. "She's in a cult in the Santa Cruz mountains that she joined when I was a little girl."

"That one where the guy sleeps with all the girls?"

"Yeah, I was meant to be one of his girls and I ran away."

"Good for you, so you kind of live on the land now?"

"So to speak. I'm not living on the Santa Monica beach or under a bridge, but I'm not living well."

"I see," he says, "Can you make me some toast?" I come back with the toast and he continues to eat fastidiously on his table on the patio. "Sit down," he says. "I'm thinking. So what about your father? Where's he?"

"He works for Goldman Sachs. My mother gave me his number. Apparently, she collected child support from him so she knows where he works. I called him and he said, *good luck*."

"That man should be ashamed of himself," Ed says. "Why don't you clean up from breakfast and let me do some research." I clean up and he goes back into his bedroom in his bathrobe, and I can hear him running the bathtub and whistling. I follow my list of instructions and water the plants, do the laundry, and dust the furniture. Ed appears an hour or so later suited up as if he's ready to go out. "You ready to go?" he asks.

"Where are we going?"

"We're going to meet your father," he says.

"What?"

"I have done some research and found out where your father lives and it's time to get him to help you support yourself. I can't have someone working for me who is homeless. I'm not going to allow it. I can't have you come and stay with me; people would say things. I'm going to shame that father of yours into doing what he should have done in the first place which is being involved in the welfare of his daughter. I am positive that when he sees you, he will invite you to stay with you. He has a big house. So don't worry about a thing."

"I'm not sure this is a good idea," I say. I really wish this guy would not get involved in my life.

"You're sure he is your father."

"Absolutely. I have my birth certificate in my car. But he isn't going to want to help me. He'll be very angry."

"That does not matter. Time for him to man up. Hop in the car. We're going." Ed's car is an Audi, and I'm pretty excited to be in a fancy car like this. I don't have any friends to impress, but I think that if I were rich, this is the kind of car I wouldn't mind driving. As we drive along, Ed keeps talking, "What's your big dream, honey? What are you going to college for?"

"I plan to get a degree in English, be a writer, maybe start my own business. I have a lot of good ideas. I might never be a fancy woman in high heels going to parties and flying to New York, but I'd like to have a successful business that would let me help a few of my friends that need help. I'm thinking businesses that come to people's houses like dog washing and house cleaning and tutoring."

"Good for you, kid." Ed drives carefully in the fancy car. He explains that he made his money in private investment banking.

"What's that?"

"That's taking care of rich people who invest their money in the stock market," he says.

"I don't know anything about the stock market except what I learned in econ class. It doesn't matter to poor people what happens in the stock market. We learned in our business class that half of Americans have some money in the stock market because of their 401Ks but only 14 percent actually buy stock, and let's face it, I'm not going to have a 401K and I'm not going to be buying stock."

"Yet here we are going to visit your father who works in the stock market."

"You know, I think this was a really bad idea."

"Maybe he'll love you."

"I doubt it," I say. I stare out the window as we drive through the gates of Bel Air which look like the entrance to some incredible off-limits kingdom.

"Don't be ridiculous," Ed says. "Listen. I'm not going to take off and leave you here. I am going to talk with him myself. But it's going to be fine. How could he not love you?" We pull up to a large house with pillars and expensive gardening, and Ed walks up with me to the door. He rings the bell. A maid answers. "We're here for Mr. Alexander," he says, "this girl's father." If the maid is surprised, she doesn't show it. She is an older white woman with pursed lips. She disappears and comes back in a few minutes.

"Welcome," she says. "Come on in." Ed steps inside and in a few moments, my father appears. He stares at Ed coldly. I am behind him. Ed taps me on the head. "It's been a while," he says putting out his hand. "This is your daughter. I thought you two should meet."

My father does not take his hand. "Please take her back wherever you found her," he says. "Her brother is a homosexual, and according to her mother, she probably is too. I don't want her. I have a wife. I have a family. Please." He raises both hands and steps back. He has not yet threatened anything. Ed doesn't speak. He turns and takes my hand as we exit the house. There is a moment when I feel the house, the crystal chandeliers, the overstuffed furniture, the kids in the backyard, and then we are gone. The Audi purrs out of the driveway. Ed doesn't speak on the way back to his house. I drive back to Topanga and instantly fall asleep and dream I am letting birds out of their cages.

CHAPTER 7

MARCH 22ND

I SLEPT OFF AND ON YESTERDAY and hiked around Topanga Park. The only food I have in my car is tuna and apples, and I need to be careful how much I eat. The money I'm making now is going to toward gas and possible car repair. I am searching online to find a Chromebook so that I can finish the semester although I'm not sure where I will get Wi-Fi. They cost almost two hundred new, but I'm finding used ones for fifty dollars. Today, I'm going to check one out.

I drive to Toluca Lake and meet a guy who has a Chromebook he hasn't even used. He says he thought it was a regular laptop but when he got it and realized it had no storage, he decided to get rid of it but then he got busy. "What do you do?" he asks.

"I do stuff for people," I say. "I wash cars, tutor kids, cook for old people, run errands, you name it."

"Wait a minute," the guy says. "I'd be happy to trade this for you detailing my BMW." He gestures toward the driveway. "Everything you need is in the garage. I need to leave in one hour."

"You got it," I say, and I go to work. I've never done this fancy of a car alone, but I figure it out, and when I'm finished, he hands me the computer and slips me a twenty.

"You want to come back and clean the car once a week?" he asks. Oddly, while I was cleaning his car, someone else on his street asked me to clean their car, so when I was finished, I cleaned their car. So now, when I come back to this neighborhood, I'll have two cars to clean.

The great thing about having the Chromebook is that he threw in a handful of flash drives. A Chromebook is no good if you have no storage, and he has no use for his flash drives, now that he has a big computer and nicer flash drives. So now, I am going to be all set for doing my school work, and I have forty dollars which will more than take care of the Saturday beer for the party. I should get something else, maybe a big bag of rice for the family. I want to help out. That forty dollars feels like it just fell out of the sky.

"Sure," I say. I drive away, thinking about rich people and how weird they are. My phone rings and it's Sally.

"Can I buy you coffee?" she says. "I have a little gift for you. My mother gave it to me, and I don't want it so I'm giving it to you. Plus, I got something else for you."

"Sure, Starbucks by your house?"

We pull up to the drive-through and there is no sign of the gift. "What do you want?" she asks. Normally, I would just say coffee black, but I decide to go big.

"Carmel frap," I say.

"So," she says. "I came home early from visiting my mama, because Mama has gone to Jesus."

"I'm sorry to hear that," I say.

"Well, it was her time. I came home early and what did I find?"

"I don't know. What did you find? A clean house?"

"I found my husband with two girls reliving his Vietnam days." I just stare at her and try to look non-committal.

"No response?"

"No, I have nothing to say."

"You were there, you saw all this going on."

"Sadly, we did."

"Did you take part?"

"Jesus no. He's not even circumcised. Sorry, that just came out."

"Was he naked when you arrived?"

"He was. But there's no way in hell I would be caught dead sleeping with him. I don't sleep with my employers or with old men. God, the very idea makes me sick. Were they being paid? We couldn't tell."

"I don't know what he promised them. Presents and trips probably. I'm going to kill him."

I lick my caramel and whipped cream with the straw. "Are you really?" I ask. "Wouldn't you go to jail?"

"No not really. I am stuck in the house with him for God knows how long with this stupid pandemic. I can't even have lunch with friends. No theater. Nothing. If you and your friend aren't coming to clean the house and at least break up my week, my life is over. Here's the deal. I want you and your friend to clean the house twice a week. We are not going to talk about what happened and I am willing to do something for you." Sally goes to her car and comes back with a bag and pulls out a small mini rice maker. "This plugs into your cigarette lighter so you can make rice in your car. I have no idea why my mother had this and gave it to me before she died, in the box unopened. I bought you this to go with it." She hands me a twenty-five-pound bag of jasmine rice.

"Wow," I say. "I can eat rice every day. This will keep me going for a long time. Thank you so much."

"You are welcome. Now I have another job for you. I am trusting you here. This is the address of the shop where I buy weed. Here is some cash. I'm over sixty so I don't want to go out right now, but I want you to pick up stuff for myself and my neighbor. If you can get the stuff on the list and bring it back to the house, I'll give you forty dollars."

"Can I go put this in the car?" I say.

"Don't ask permission," she says. "Just do it." When I get back, we're both still finishing our frozen coffee.

"So, what's your plan? I get Sophia, but you?"

"I'm going to college. I hope to have a better job. I doubt I've ever have a bespoke suit, but I won't always be poor."

"Rich people are born rich, I'm sorry to tell you. But do what you can. A lot of poor people get into trouble. Try to stay out of trouble."

"I can think of some poor people who have made it around the world."

"They were the exceptions. The rule is that you work for other people, you get trampled. Enjoy your rice. I'll have your money when you get back with the weed. And next time my husband is whoring around, call me."

"Thanks for the coffee and the rice," I say.

"I own your ass," she says. "Don't forget." I can't wait to try the little rice cooker. The idea of having a bowl of rice every day seems way too exciting. But now I'm going to have to rat out Chuck. The things we do for rice.

MY PHONE RINGS AT EIGHT IN the morning. I'm walking around the park getting ready to buy coffee. What I found out about the little rice maker last night is that it takes twenty-five minutes to make rice. That means about one to two dollars of gas which is not a good deal. This means I have to run the rice cooker while I'm driving back to Topanga or I don't get to eat. No dinner last night except the apples I always keep in my car. I read some more of my Lorrie Moore book. People give me books all the time. I will take any book. I give them away to other un-housed people if they have enough of a situation where they can keep books for a while.

"Could you get over?" Ed says. "I think I sprained my ankle. I need you here every day. I don't know why you aren't here."

"Okay," I say. "I don't know that I can do every day."

"Just get over here." I find him on the floor in the living room. His leg looks bad.

"Why didn't you call 911? I'm pretty sure this is what 911 was invented for."

"No, it is not; 911 is when you walk in on some guy murdering his wife or selling cocaine out of your kitchen. You know one time I walked in on a guy who had handcuffed a girl to the bed, and I was about to call 911, and it turned out to be their thing."

"Okay, that sounds terrific. Let's get you in your car and then you can tell me why you were you walking in on people having sex play. Because I'm pretty sure you're supposed to knock." He's heavier than he looks, but I get him into his car, and he hands me the keys.

"Drive carefully. We're going to Cedars. My brother is a doctor there, so he'll make sure I am taken care of. I'm calling him now." I can hear him on the phone because the phone is part of the car. "I slipped and fell making coffee. Yeah, my maid is out of town. When she comes back, damn the coronavirus, I'm having her come back to take care of me. I can't be expected to do everything. It's ridiculous. Who's driving me now? My errand girl Mia. We'll be there shortly, but I'll need a wheelchair. It wasn't easy getting me into the car."

He doesn't say anything, just stares out the window. He turns on the opera station. "My brother and I don't speak unless we need to. Do you like opera?"

I was about to say. "Does anyone like opera?" Because somehow in my head it was all shouting, but what comes on is this one beautiful melody. "I like this," I say.

"Everyone likes this," he says. "This is *Carmen* sung by Leontyne Price. She had quite a voice. You know when she first started her career, they told her shouldn't sing white roles."

"Jesus," I say, "with a voice like that, she could sing God," I'm almost crying in the car driving along. How has my generation, lost in Gaga and hip hop never listened to this woman? All I want to do is listen to Leontyne Price.

At the hospital, I'm surprised at how well my employer is treated. They meet the car with a wheelchair. I've brought my book along, and I find a place to curl up, but he's back with me in a couple of hours in a leg brace. The brother who is younger than Ed comes out to talk with me. "Ed says you'll be looking after him," he says. I look to the right and left for help. "And staying with him," the doctor adds "to make sure he's okay."

"I don't know," I say. "Maybe the housekeeper is coming back."

"She's stuck in El Salvador because of Covid. She needs permission from the state department to get back and she won't be back until April 15th at least. Now according to Ed, you aren't staying anywhere right now, so this will be perfect for you. You can leave during the day to do your other jobs, but you will make sure Ed gets up in the morning and gets breakfast, leave him his lunch and get home in time to make him dinner, and I need you to look out for him. Is that clear."

"Okay," I say. What I'm thinking is that I better be paid, because we are not friends. When we start driving, I say, "Wow, that was bossy. I don't like being bossed around by your doctor."

"Doctors are bossy. They think they're God. Ever heard of the M. Deity complex? Well, they have it. So let me ask you, can you take care of me? I suppose having a place to stay for the next few weeks isn't a terrible idea?"

"If we're doing this, we need to make a deal. Here's what I need. I need to use the Wi-Fi to finish my classes while I'm at your house. Once I'm out, I'll go back to squatting by Starbucks. I won't eat your food. I have my own food which I can make for myself. I need to go out to jobs during the day. And I do need to be paid."

"Just a question, none of my business, but do you put your money in a bank?"

"No, I keep it all in my sock and spend the rest on weed. Yes, I put every cent in the bank. I'm saving."

"When we get home, I want to know why you aren't taking out student loans like a normal person."

"Wow, how much pain medicine did they give you?"

"Enough."

We get him into the house and settled on his couch in the living room. This house was professionally decorated years ago, he's told me, and the paintings, furniture, and rugs all have a mixture of reds and blacks. When I described the house to Sally, she said, it was probably an East Coast designer. I like it. "Explain the student loans or lack thereof," he says.

"Getting student loans without your parents is not impossible but it helps if you have credit which I don't. If you have no credit as in you've never had any credit at all and you have no parents you are going to get the worst possible rate on student loans and when you graduate, you will have at least fifty thousand in debt, and because I am a poor person with no job prospects, I will have difficulty in paying them back. I talked with someone in the counseling office when I was getting started. She had a PhD from a private school which she had finished fifteen years before. She was making a good salary as a counselor. She was making payments on her student loans. She pulled them up for me. When she had graduated at age forty, she owed $135,000. Fifteen years later, she owed $138,000. I was looking over her shoulder at her account. I could see it and I knew I would live in my car before I would do that to myself. The amount she owed is the cost of a house in most of the country. There are forty-five million people who owe 1.6 trillion and no matter what you do, it never gets paid off. My employer Sally says that I will always be poor and without bespoke suits. That may be true, but I will also be without student loan debt."

"Okay, let's say, you can finish school here. You can do your homework when you come by to run errands. It's bad enough that you don't get to see your classmates and you don't get to walk around campus. What kind of a college life are you having? I don't like the thought of you crouching outside a Starbucks leaning on their Wi-Fi. As far as food, what food are you planning to eat?"

"I have a bag of rice."

"What would you eat with the rice if you could eat anything?"

"Well, I would eat fruit for breakfast and avocados, green onions, and sriracha sauce. But I'm fine with just rice. I really am."

"Okay, you are the worst bargainer in the world. You have a man who literally has no other options. You could ask for the moon. I'm going to bargain for you a little here.

When you go to the store, I'm going to insist you buy the stuff you want for yourself, and we will make this work for both of us."

"I have one question," I say and then I can get going on dinner. "Can we listen to some more of that singer, Leontyne Price?"

CHAPTER 8

APRIL 3RD

SHERYL WAKES UP ON THE FIRST day that mask wearing is announced with the worst hangover she's ever had. She reaches for her phone and speed dials Ivy. Ivy answers on the first ring. "Ivy, I need help, I'm hungover."

"Gotcha," Ivy says and she knows help is on the way. She lies back and breathes. In less than an hour the door opens and Ivy's face appears framed by light. Ivy works quickly, she sets up her IV drip bag and has anti-nausea and pain meds dripping into her vein. When the bag's empty, she feels like moving again. Ivy's moving for the door.

"I'll Venmo you," she says.

"You might want to call for help with the boys," Ivy says. "Just saying." And then she's gone.

Sheryl can feel the combination of magnesium, pain meds, and anti-nausea drugs smoothing everything down in her system. She can't remember how she stayed alive without this. Sheryl tries to remember last night. Things have gone steadily downhill since Richard moved closer to the hospital because he was worried about infecting the family.

"You'll be fine," he'd said. "Just supervise their schoolwork and then let them play in the afternoon." The boys waved to him when he pulled out of the driveway, and then they turned to her and laughed. Since then, they have simply done whatever they wanted. They've done no schoolwork at all. She called the school to say that they are very ill and may need to take an incomplete on the semester. They order pizza every day, swim in the pool, play video games, and watch porn. All she can think is that she's happy they aren't having weed delivered or having girls show up at the door to entertain them. They ignore anything she says to them.

She had asked them to pick up pizza boxes and to help her with the laundry, and they began screaming at her that she was a useless twat. "Idiot," one said. "Useless twat," the other added. "Bimbo," the first one said, then they were both at it, "Bimbo, bimbo. Bimbo." What was funny is that Sheryl runs her own business. She has an MBA; she hangs with a bimbo crowd and dyes her hair blond and gets injections to fit in with the lounge crowd, but she never really does, and she feels like her sons are seeing into her heart.

When she first got married, she'd thought she had it all, the house, the handsome doctor husband, a job she liked, friends. Her life was spectacular, like a beach sunset. Sometimes she got twinges around the edges. When the kids came, at first, it seemed okay. It wasn't until they were three or four, that it became obvious that she wasn't a good mother.

But still, they had school, activities, babysitters, she was almost never alone with them. She kept thinking they would grow out of it. She was always going to tell Richard and have him help her figure it out.

She went to the kitchen last night and poured herself a vodka and then took the whole bottle into her bedroom and locked the door. That's how she ended up this morning with a hangover that required Ivy. She needs to go back to Ivy coming to the house every month. She's falling apart.

She is raising psychopaths; it's time to ignore her husband and ask for help. She calls Mia.

"MIA," SHERYL SAYS ON THE PHONE. "I need help with the boys. I miss you. Could you come over?" I feel like I am sliding from one desperate person to another, just as I am not sure if I can feed myself or save for my UCLA tuition, another person calls me. I go to sleep every night after doing my homework wondering if I am going to make it through next week. I think about money all the time.

"Let me check and call you back." I'm finishing with Ed's breakfast.

"Who was that?" he says.

"This woman I used to babysit for. She fired me as soon as Covid happened and she tried to get me to video chat with her sons, but now she wants me back because she's a terrible parent, and her husband's probably at the hospital all the time and she needs help."

"Sounds simple. Sounds like a job."

"This woman isn't my friend."

"Of course, she isn't your friend. I'm not your friend. I'm your employer. And here's the deal, honey. If you had a parent with any money, you would be living with them. They would help you go to college. If you had a friend who cared about you and wasn't Salvadoran and living in a crowded apartment, you'd be staying with them. You don't have any friends. You have your Salvadoran friends, and you have employers. It's confusing because you were in her home taking care of her children; that's intimate and it feels like she should care about your welfare, but she doesn't even see you except in the ways you can make her life better. You are like the doorman at the hotel or the waiter at the restaurant. Some people are kinder than others. I get that she isn't very kind. And you are taking care of her children. I want you to know that as for me, I appreciate you. Go do this job. And, you'll be doing the kids a favor too. It sounds like the kids need a steady hand."

I call her back. "I'll be right over," I say. When I get to the house, Luke and Matthew are waiting for me. "What have you two monsters been up to?" I ask.

"Watching porn, playing video games. Doing no schoolwork!" they say.

"Why are you guys such monsters to your mama?"

"We don't know," they say together.

"Well, sit down, buckle up, because you two are going to start catching up on school right about now." They seem relieved that someone is there to put the brakes on the madness. I contact their school; say they are feeling better and get them going on their homework. I clean up the house. Sheryl comes downstairs in her bathrobe while I'm cleaning.

"I'm so glad to see you. We've missed you. Haven't we missed you boys?" They glare at her. I don't say anything. I'm not going to mediate what goes on between them and their mother. If I can get them caught up on their school and get this house in order, that's enough.

She makes coffee and stares out at the pool drinking cup after cup and then goes up to take a long bath while I keep cleaning. When I've finished, we agree that I'll come back three days a week and on the other days I'll zoom with the boys to make sure they do their school, and she'll pay me for five days.

"You've saved my life," she says. "I want to give something to you, you've been amazing." She goes into her closet and comes out with a dress. "I want to give this to you. I've worn it a few times and I don't wear it anymore. It's too big on me. I think it could work on you. You can wear it to anything. It's kind of yacht party kind of dress, but seriously, you could wear it to any kind of summer party."

I thank her and I drive to the Buffalo Exchange in Sherman Oaks. I hold out the dress which is three sizes too large for me. "How much?" I ask. "It's a designer thing."

"I'll give you eleven dollars," the girl says and my heart sinks. I know it's worth more than that, but where else am I selling it? I could try the Buffalo Exchange on Melrose, but they may not be better. I pocket the eleven dollars and go back to the house on Mulholland Drive. The old man wants salmon for dinner. I google "baked salmon recipes." He says my martinis are improving. I'm getting the dirty part.

He never explained about walking in on the couple with handcuffs. I wonder if that was his ex-wife. I wonder if he'll

ever tell me. Maybe not since we aren't friends. I like my dinners of rice and avocado, green onion and sriracha, I can't
feel my ribs so much now. I even swim in the old man's pool
at night. All this is temporary. Soon, I'll be turned out into
the night.

CHAPTER 9

─────

APRIL 4TH

I HAVE NEVER BEEN HAPPIER TO have Saturday come around. My Saturday evenings at Sophia's family's house are the brightest spot of my week. I show up with the Dos Equis and since Covid, I bring food as well. Sophia's daughter lost her job at Pierce. Roberto is a landscaper, so they still have his income and Sophia's, but they count on all three incomes, and they have the baby, Juan, who we call Suave because he has his moves and so many smiles he gets us to hold him all the time. Sophia's daughter Olivia and I met when she was pregnant, and one night she told me the whole story of how she got pregnant, but it isn't something their family spends any time talking about.

SOPHIA, ROBERTO, AND OLIVIA ALL WORKED at a house in Calabasas. Olivia and Sophia cleaned the house and Roberto was the gardener and cleaned the cars. One of the sons was always talking with Olivia while she did the house cleaning and telling her how cute she was and how he wanted to take her on a trip. Finally one Friday, Sophia was out sick and he was there alone when Olivia was and he convinced her to take a trip with him to Santa Barbara. On the way up the coast, he told her that he was in love, that he wanted to take her to Paris, that they would get married and spend their lives together. He kept telling tales, and her head was spinning. She'd heard some of the moves from the boys in her neighborhood, but never the storied lines from the polished throat of a rich white boy. Even when she was telling me this, I thought that I too would have swallowed it all like eating cake for the first time in your life, the soft sweetness and the frosting of those words would have slid down my throat. He was playing music in the car. *What's this music?* she asked. And he said, *It's Dean Martin singing "Sway with Me,"* and she was all in.

They stayed that night at a fancy hotel by the sea and she lost her virginity. In the morning, he said he had to go golfing and meet people for dinner, so he took her to Union Station. It was a long ride to the station, more than two hours, and when her parents arrived at that cathedral of a train station in bustling downtown Los Angeles, they didn't ask a thing. There was just waiting for one month, then two. She did not go back to clean that house. She got the job at Pierce and asked me to take over cleaning. Sophia still washes that boy's underwear when he comes home from college.

When I hear politicians say that Latinos are lazy, I think of that family in that tiny apartment, that little Juan; they never told that wealthy family in Calabasas; Sophia just kept cleaning. I see Nick from time to time. Once he came over to talk to me. Sophia walked over to him, "We're here to work," she said looking him straight in the eyes. He backed away, something about her frightened him.

AT SOPHIA'S HOUSE, I'VE BROUGHT A stack of corn tortillas and a chicken. Sophia shoos me into the living room with lime and a beer so she can take charge of her tiny kitchen and Roberto begins to hold forth on the essence of class struggle in the Americas. We, the daughters, often have to disagree with some of his opinions. He's a bit of a Marxist. He thinks that eventually people in America will be sick of the trillion plus in student loan debt and will demand free universities and that with free universities we wouldn't have this big division between the haves and have-nots.

Olivia and I see things differently. We think the revolution that happened where women got the vote was because men cared enough about women, and the Civil Rights Act of 1964 happened because at least some white people wanted African Americans to be treated equally. We don't think rich people in the US care about anyone but themselves otherwise why would the rich keep making sure that generational wealth keeps getting passed on, that there are no taxes on inheritance, and that there are more billionaires every year? Why are the rich barely taxed in this country? "Rich people don't care about poor people," we tell him.

At this point, Roberto would begin to cut in and say that the Constitution does not do anything about police brutality against people of color in cities across America. This is one of his favorite subjects of conversation, that equal rights should mean equal right to safety, equal rights to good schools, and equal rights to health care. We have great conversations, and I'm usually at their house until midnight. I nurse one beer and then switch to coffee. I love spending time with Juan, and I want to make sure Sophia and Roberto will make it through this crisis. It's hard for families with no savings. Sophia has lost quite a few of her jobs, so they are scraping along. I am bringing them food every week. I brought them a large bag of rice, dry beans, and I also get onions, celery, and peppers. You can live on surprisingly little if you are able to cook. The diapers for the baby really bite, but now that I go to Costco for some of my clients, I buy diapers there. We usually end the evening singing, and if you ask us, we are wonderful singers.

CHAPTER 10

APRIL 6TH

I'M AT CEDARS WITH ED WHEN my phone rings. It's Sophia.

"It's an emergency."

"Okay, give me a second. He's going in with his doctor— okay here I am. What's up?"

"I'm worried that I might have Covid."

"Why what happened?"

"You know that guy Nick that got Olivia pregnant? Well, I'm still cleaning that family's house as you know, and I've been cleaning it by myself, it just takes longer, and Nick called me today to say that he wanted me to know that he tested positive last Thursday, and he still had me come clean the house Friday because he was going to have a party at the house on the weekend. He also wants me to come clean up the house after the party."

"This guy is a goddamn idiot."

"I said, why didn't you tell me before I came to the house, and he just said, well, I was asymptomatic, so I didn't think I was going to get you sick and it wasn't like we were going to have sex or anything and then he laughed like that was funny."

"That little fuck face. Where are his parents?"

"I don't know. Around. I think they golf mostly. They are the ones that pay me."

"Are you sick?"

"No, but I'm worried about you. You just stopped by."

"I hadn't even thought about myself. I'm at a hospital, I'm going to see if they will test me. You take care of you. I'll call you back after I get tested."

"I need someone to go clean my client's house."

"Let me call you back," I say. "How's Roberto?"

"He's fine. We both need to get tested. But I'm going to lose a couple weeks of work."

"Go get tested and then, just rest," I say. "I'll call you back."

Ed manages to convince Cedars that they should test me as his caretaker, and I come out negative for Covid. We drive back to his house stopping for smoked salmon, berries, crème fraiche, and some microgreens. I'm learning how rich people like to eat. It's expensive, but it looks good. The next morning, I make him breakfast and then go to Vallarta for Mexican bread, eggs, avocados, tamales, and fresh salsa and drop it off to Sophia and Roberto. They've all gone for testing including the baby.

While I'm there, sitting in the courtyard of their apartment complex, Sophia tells me that Nick's mother is calling to say that they've got Nick staying at an Airbnb and they want to know if I will come clean the house. I tell Sophia, I can take Juan with me in a playpen so they can rest, and they get the car seat ready and I take off.

At the Royal house, I get the playpen set up for Juan and get going on cleaning. I can't listen to my tunes because I have to listen for the baby, but I'm rocking through the cleaning when Mrs. Royal appears in her silk pajamas. She oohs and aahs over Juan. She even goes and gets a stuffed animal from somewhere and gives Juan a blue elephant. I get the house done in five hours, scrubbing and cleaning, do the laundry, getting all the recycling out to the blue trash can, wiping the counters, cleaning up after what must have been a big party. I keep thinking of Sophia and Roberto, home on the couch watching Star Trek working on their American English, "Beam me up, Scotty," they say together. I feel anger boiling inside me, but it does no good. Getting angry is like blowing in the wind; it's useless.

Mrs. Royal comes out to pay me. "Sit down for a moment," she says laying out the one hundred and fifty on the table. "You are friends with Sophia?"

"Yes." I almost say, "I'm giving this money to her," but I remember what I always tell myself, "Never trust rich people. Anything you say they'll use against you. Especially anything personal."

"Whose baby is this?"

"Sophia's grandson."

"Olivia's son?"

"Yes." She sits there quietly pursing her lips, and she narrows her eyes for a moment.

"I see," she says. "You seem angry."

"I'm not angry," I say. What I'm thinking is, *For me to be angry at you, I'd have to have a voice in this conversation, and this isn't even a conversation because we don't speak the same language or live in the same world or breathe the same air.* Sophia said to keep my head down and my mouth shut.

"Just a moment," Mrs. Royal says. She disappears into the kitchen and rummages in her purse and comes back with another hundred. "Tell Sophia this is to help with the income she's losing during quarantine and with the baby," she says. "I would give you more, but you people don't know how to save. I know you spend money as soon as you see it, so maybe next week, I can give you more. Tell Sophia we'll help out. I want things to be okay. I mean, I have to ask myself what people like you think is happening when you go off somewhere with someone like Nick? Grow up. I'll help out as long as she stays where she is. I don't want you people moving in next door."

"I think you're safe," I say. "I don't think Sophia can afford this neighborhood."

"Of course not," Mrs. Royal laughs. "You get along home now to Sophia and then to your parents. At least you aren't a spoiled little brat. I bet your parents make sure you don't climb into cars with strangers."

"Nick wasn't a stranger. He said he loved her. He said he was taking her to Paris. He said they were going to get married."

"Be quiet." At that moment, Juan screams, and I run to him; I grab him up, fold the playpen in one hand, grab my stuff in the other and I am out the door. She comes to the door. "You watch yourself," she says.

"No, you watch yourself," I say. She comes to the car to make sure I know how to put Juan in his car seat. "I'm out of line," I say.

"Emotions run high," she says. I'm always amazed at how rich people can smooth things over, like they're born with smooth lines. I keep thinking that she is well brought up and that I most certainly am not. She keeps looking at the baby, and then she waves to me. I drive away with her only grandchild.

CHAPTER 11

APRIL 12TH

I SHOW UP TO TAKE CARE of the twins on Easter, and their mom has all the stuff laid out for me. She's drinking champagne and eating berries while I supervise them painting eggs. While they're doing the painting, I sneak out in the yard and hide the eggs and make their baskets which consist of a lot of chocolate. I've bought myself Starbucks so I'm drinking my coffee and having a good time with them while she drinks her champagne and zooms with her friends. "I've got a surprise for you this afternoon," she says.

I get a cold feeling thinking about this surprise. This woman has no idea what kind of thing I might want so what kind of surprise would she get for me? The boys find the eggs and settle in to eat the chocolate and go for a swim while I clean up. When they come in from the pool, I get them settled in their room playing *Call of Duty Black Ops*.

Sitting by the pool are eight kids my age. "Is this the surprise?" I ask.

"Yes," Sheryl says. "Grab a beer, this is my gift to you. I get the feeling you never get to socialize with people your own age." All of the kids are pretty fashionably dressed, and I am wearing cutoff shorts, a tank top, and flip flops. My hair is uncut and down to my waist; I haven't had a haircut for years. I don't wear makeup; I don't have any jewelry except some bracelets I made myself. These are private school kids. This is horrible and humiliating. I want to leave. "Go on. You can do this." I get a beer and go outside and sit down.

"Hey, what's your name?" Blondie says.

"Mia."

"So, you're the kids' babysitter?" She asks.

"Yeah."

"So, we were just talking about where we buy weed."

"I buy weed at Exhalence," I say. "I buy it for a bunch for old people who are afraid to go out and buy their own stuff because of Covid. They have a hydroponics place in the back, and they grow it there as well."

"Sounds rad." The boys are listening too. Score, I think. Conversation point.

One of the boys is staring at his phone. "Are you following this?" he says. "It's trending on Twitter." He hands his phone to one of the girls.

They all read and then one of them says, "Have you seen this TikTok?" and she passes it around and she passes it to me as well. I've never seen anything on TikTok. At night before I go to sleep, I read. I don't play on my phone. I know everyone of my generation plays on their phones. But I'm not really of my generation. I'm poor and I don't have time to do TikTok or Twitter or social media.

"Shall we swim?" I ask.

"Do you have a suit?"

"No."

"You could swim naked."

"Betts is in a polyamorous relationship, so she goes naked all the time at her house."

The blond girl laughs. "Well, we're not at my house." She smiles. "My dad bought me a house in Sherman Oaks, and I live there with my husband and my girlfriend, and we are poly at least for now."

"Who is allowed to do what?" I ask.

"We have a bit of a throuple going and we are allowed to explore outside our marriage as well."

"I see," I say, although I don't. "Why get married if you aren't into monogamy?"

"Parents wanted me to get married; it was the only way they would buy me a house."

"Gotcha. And you like girls and boys."

"What about you? Boys? Girls?"

One of the boys cuts in, "Don't bug her Betts," before I can answer which is just as well because I think both, but I'm not sure. "Just jump in the pool with your clothes on," the boy says, and I do.

AT THE END OF THE AFTERNOON, I thank Sheryl for the little get together, and I check the boys before I leave. I've set up a tent for them in their living room in front of the game console so they can sleep in sleeping bags in the tent and watch the TV until they fall asleep. They're just falling asleep when I go in, "Good night you princes of Maine, you kings of New England," I say.

"You always say that" they say. "Why can't we be kings be from California?"

"Because it's from *The Cider House Rules*," I say. "Okay, I'll change it. Good night you princes of Calabasas, you kings of California."

"Much better," they say, and fall asleep in the blue-green light of the television. I drive home to the old man who is probably ready for his dinner. I think about what I have learned tonight. These rich kids were nice. I've learned about throuples, adding a unicorn to your couple, trending on Twitter, and quite a bit about smoking six-foot bongs, eating shrooms, and going skiing in Mammoth, something they all seem to have done quite a bit. Their lives are so different than mine; they could be a different species, but they came down from their planet and for a brief moment we spoke the same language.

CHAPTER 12

APRIL 13TH

IT'S A RELIEF THAT SOPHIA AND Roberto didn't get Covid, but I still am angry at Nick for his carelessness. Sophia gets the flu which turns out not to be Covid, so she misses work anyway. I get a call from Mrs. Royal. She sounds frantic. I can hear her screaming and yelling but I can't make out what she's talking about. I put her on speaker phone. "What do I do?" I mouth to Ed.

"Wait," he says. "Put the phone on mute. Okay, this isn't your friend. This is your employer. Wait until she settles down and then find out the problem and see if she needs to call 911. You are not driving over there unless you are being paid to do a job. You are not driving over there to listen to that."

I wait. Eventually the hysteria settles. "What can I do for you?" I say, "Because I understand that you're upset, but I'm not sure I know what the problem is."

"I want you to come over here right now to help clean the house. I can pay you."

"Okay, what was all the screaming?"

"I'm very upset today."

"I'll be over."

When I pull into the driveway, Mrs. Royal meets me in the doorway. "Nick's girlfriend is dead," she says. "She's out in the pool house."

"Have you called the police?"

"No, they'll take him away. We are not calling the police. We are going to bury her."

"Okay, where is Mr. Royal?"

"He had to go to Washington."

"Where's Nick?"

"Passed out cold."

"You seem calmer than when we talked on the phone," I say. She seems very calm in fact.

"I have taken quite a few Xanax," she says and slips to the floor. I cover her with a blanket and get a pillow. I go to the phone and call 911. I report an emergency a possible homicide, and woman who will need her stomach pumped. Then I look for Mrs. Royal's phone and I call her husband. Mr. Royal answers the phone.

"Hello Mr. Royal," I say.

"Who's this?"

"The cleaning girl, Mia."

"Why are you calling from my wife's phone?"

"I just arrived at the house. Your wife called me hysterical; she asked me if she could pay me to clean the house. I came here to find her looped on Xanax. I'm now walking out to the pool house where it looks like young Nick is passed out and his girlfriend, it's hard to say if she alive but I'm sure they'll figure that out shortly. I called the police."

"See if she's breathing."

"Okay, fingers to pulse here, I'm going to say that's a no. Pretty cold. Nick seems okay though."

"Any idea why she died?"

I am keeping myself calm. "Hard to say, I don't see a gun, I don't want to interfere with the scene here. No gun obvious. No blood. I'm going to guess, drugs? I don't know how to put the alarm on your house sir, so after everyone is taken away, you want me to just lock up?"

"I'll pay you for today. You Venmo?"

"Yes sir."

"Write down my number and send me your Venmo information. Call me back as soon as the cops arrive, I want to speak to them. Do you understand what I'm saying? You will call me when you lock up the house, I'll tell you how to lock up. Are we clear. If I am going to pay you, all this needs to be done."

"Yes sir," I say.

The young woman's body was stiff and unyielding. She was wearing a white dress, and her sandals had been kicked off. I didn't see any needles or drugs, but the door was open into the bedroom of the pool house. The police arrive and they take my statement and then Mr. Royal gets on the phone and gives a statement as well. They take Nick and his mother in an ambulance, and I have to wait three more hours for the coroner to come for the girl's body. I am sitting outside while they zip the girl's body into the body bag. Her hair is red. No one is ever going to tell me what happened to that girl. Mr. Royal walks me through their security system and five hours after I arrived, I pull out the gate.

When I get back to Ed's house, there is a text to me from Mr. Royal. "Do not talk to the media. Is that clear?" In my Venmo account he has put five hundred dollars which I think is a ridiculous amount. I wonder what the Royals will do for the girl's family. I try not to think about it.

That night, I make Ed a recipe I've found online that I've been wanting to try. It's a watermelon feta salad and with it I make barbecued chicken. I end up making too much salad because it's easy to go overboard with watermelon, and he says, "Why don't you sit down and have some of this water-melon and chicken," and for the first time we have dinner together and we listen to *Carmen*. "Rough day," he says. "Why don't you go for a swim, I'll clean up."

"No," I say, "that's crazy."

He waves his hands and I back out of the house. I dive into the pool with the palm trees above me and imagine that I am loved, that I am sheltered, that I live in the land of sunshine, that I eat honey for breakfast every morning. I swim strokes back and forth in the pool and tell myself stories in which after this house, I find another home and they love me there. They take me in, and I take care of everyone there so well that they keep me like a pet dog or parakeet, and at first they feed me seeds but eventually they feed me the real food and then I get to read all the books in the library, and some day, I get treated like those kids at the party. Someone says, "You can have any kind of relationship you want to." Someone tries to help me get jobs. I'm not flopping around like a fish on the dock. I'm swimming.

Sally tells me that men never help women get jobs unless you sleep with them. She says men pass around meat and potatoes to each other and by that she means stuff that matters. She says women pass around fruit and flowers to each other, stuff that doesn't matter. Women will offer you a dress or a pair of shoes or a walk around the park or goddamn coaching. Men have jobs they could give you that would help you live indoors. They have cars and keys and houses, but they won't give you any of that stuff unless you fuck them, and you seem afraid to fuck so you're out in the cold where the girls who don't fuck live. I want to believe that Sally's wrong. I'll meet a person who is outside gender who will help me up the stairs. Or maybe I'll build my own goddamn stairs into the sky. Either way, I'll find the sky.

CHAPTER 13

APRIL 15TH

I WAKE UP WEDNESDAY AND REMEMBER this is my day to clean Chuck and Sally's house and then I am going over to take care of the twins. I like waking up in a bed with sheets and a comforter. I lie in bed for an extra minute. The room I sleep in is a loft. I'm looking up at the peaked roof and out my window there are birds. I've hung a bird feeder, so birds are right outside my window. I haven't unpacked. I keep one bag with my stuff and every day I take my stuff with me to my car when I leave, but I like to imagine that Ed decides he wants to adopt me or something. I make breakfast and do a quick cleaning of the pool. I find a dead bird, so I get the pool cleaner going.

When I arrive at Chuck and Sally's, I hear the piano playing. She doesn't play much, so I'm surprised, but she's playing something rather loudly. I knock even though the door is open and then I go in as I always do on Wednesdays and there's Chuck dressed in a boa on the couch and she's playing away on the piano.

"Excuse me," I say. "I can come back another time," and Sally says, "Don't be silly, we'll take this party outside," and I think, is it a party when you only have two people? But they both go outside and then I hear her playing music on their stereo and he gets a towel and starts bringing drinks and I keep my head down and clean the house and then he finally disappears into the man cave, and she comes to find me. She flops down on the couch and lights a joint while I put away the dishes.

"We are on the mend," she says. "We are whistling Dixie."

"I don't think that means what you think it means," I say.

"What I mean is that we are doing the beast with two backs. We needed to get past vanilla sex. I just didn't realize that was the problem. We're not pegging or anything, but we're getting into some impact stuff and some bondage and we're bringing back the old sauce."

"That sounds fantastic. Should I skip cleaning the man cave?"

"Yeah, he's passed out. We did some benzos before we got started so he's probably sleeping very comfortably." It crosses my mind that these people are old to be smoking weed, doing street drugs, and tying each other down and spanking each other, but who am I to judge? They probably find me boring.

"Let me make us some coffee," she says. "Where are you going next?"

"Calabasas," I say.

"Still staying with the old guy?"

"Yeah."

"Has he tried any funny business?" She makes a sandwich of turkey, provolone, lettuce, and tomatoes and offers me half.

"Are you sure?" I ask.

"Yes, I'm sure." I try to eat it slowly. It is a tasty sandwich. When I was at the party the other day, one of the girls was telling everyone that she was vegan. I can't be vegan. I'm too poor to be vegan. I haven't had anything to eat today so if someone offers me a sandwich, I am going to eat it. I've never had veal or lamb, and I don't know if I could bear that. I also have never had any pork or red meat, but this sandwich is delicious and if a person offered me pizza with pepperoni, I would not turn it down. Sadly no one is offering.

"Are you hoping he'll save you?"

"No, I'm saving him. I'm rescuing him. His housekeeper is out of town."

"Aren't you kind of hoping she doesn't come back, that maybe he'll see how wonderful you are and decide to adopt you or something?"

"Orphans are invisible. Nobody sees us and there's no place worse than Los Angeles. I didn't realize it when I came down from the Bay Area, I was living up there with a group of gay kids who had been turned out by their parents and they were super cool. Here I haven't made a single friend except Olivia and her family. This is a city that eats you up and vomits you out. Look at all these homeless people. You can die in Los Angeles lying against the shining palm trees in Santa Monica. I help a lot of people; I am the one who helps people all the time. People call me for help. When my phone rings, someone wants help. No one saves the savior. No one thinks, I wonder, how she's doing? How is she making it? How is she building her own cathedral of the soul?"

Sally goes to her cupboard. She hands me a chocolate bar. "Something for the road," she says. I like this new side of her all kinky, stoned, and happy. Usually she listens to Fox News and stares at television.

Most people when I come to their houses, are watching news about the president. Whether they like him or not, they are obsessively watching him. I keep wondering if he doesn't get elected, what will occupy our darkened national consciousness so swamped by this one looming presence. He's caused a terrible freeway accident that we can't take our eyes away from. When I hear her husband talk about "libtards," and I hear the liberals afraid that another four years of Trump could ruin the world, I wonder if Americans are divided by class, color, and truth. My truth is so different from Chuck's truth, that I, little libtard that I am, cannot even understand him when he tells me what America means.

WHEN I ARRIVE AT SHERYL'S HOUSE, the twins are waiting for me in the driveway. "Mama's sleeping," they say. "I don't know if she's okay."

I don't want to ask how much she had to drink so I say, "Why don't you two clean up your room and I'll be right there." I'm hoping she's alive, and she is. I touch her neck and she's got a steady pulse going. I try to think of who I could call. Her husband is probably a bad idea. I cover her up and look around to determine how much alcohol she's drunk. It looks like maybe a bottle of wine and some vodka. I make lunch for the boys, and we work on homework and then they swim. When I'm getting ready to leave, she wakes up. "I didn't know whether to call your husband," I say. "I was worried about you."

"Never call him," she says. "He'll kill me."

"Understood," I say.

"Is there any chance you could move in for a while," she says. "I can't handle this anymore."

"I don't know how much longer my employer wants me staying with him, but can I call you tomorrow?" I say. "What if I just come over as much as I can?"

"I'll pay you," she begs. "Whatever other people are paying you, I'll pay you more."

"Okay, let me find out," I say. I don't want to leave my lovely little bird house in the sky to move in with this needy drunk woman and her two boys although the money might be better. But she'll use me up. It will be so hard to get out and do other jobs and I would be waiting on her hand and foot. I can't even imagine how horrible my life would be, but I don't how long Ed will have me. I get back to his house and I get my game on in the cooking department and bake some wild salmon and make an arugula salad and he invites me to have dinner with him. I pour him wine although I just have water. I don't want to presume too much. For dessert, he likes berries and cream. We are listening to Beethoven while I clean up, and he's explaining to me the reasons for the twelve-year war in El Salvador when there's a knock on the door. So few people knock during Covid that we both jump.

I open the door to Juanita. She rushes into the house. "Mr. Michaelsen," she says. "Are you okay? I am so sorry I was gone so long. The state department would not let me back in the US What happened to you?"

"I fell and Mia has been taking care of me. But I am so glad you were able to get back into the country, and now that you are here, I am going to bed. It's been a long day. Good night to both of you." He disappears into his bedroom at the end of the long hallway.

"Have you been staying here?"

"He asked me to."

"As you know, I don't drive him around, so come by twice a week or whenever he needs you for errands and doctor visits. See you." By some weird intuition, I had not brought my bag into the house.

I drive my car to the old lady's property in Topanga and as I get there, I see her car arriving as well. She waves to me to follow her to the main house. I've never been to her house, and when I get there, it's a piece of some strange mystical, perhaps even medieval, world. There are benches around a fire pit, and the woman herself with her strange eyes and thick gray hair looks like someone who would be entrusted with the soul of the planet. "Child," she says. "I have need of you."

Oh, my goodness, I think, *if one more person has need of me, I think I'm going to collapse. How did I come to Los Angeles this desperately poor and become someone that everyone feels they can make use of?*

"I need you to get my groceries," she says.

"That's easy," I say. "Usually, people have me get weed, and I was buying you weed a few months ago."

"Weed would be great," she says and peels off another stack of twenties. "By the weekend is fine. And child, this land is the land of the Tongva people, but it is also my home and your home, park here anytime. I will pray for you." She puts her hands on me and I swear I feel like life force is pouring into me.

It's like a jolt. I stay up late and pound through my homework, and turn it in. I'm starting to feel like I might make it through this pandemic. I have my stack of masks. I am getting used to buying weed for everyone. And, I have a car that still runs.

I wake up in my car the next day, and I have her money, so I bounce out to do the grocery run and I do the weed run for her and the old folks on Chuck and Sally's Street. I miss cleaning with Sophia. I take some money and food by their house and then I head out to Sheryl's house.

When I arrive, she's half hammered and sitting by the pool. "Ma'am," I say.

"Call me Sheryl," she says swishing her feet around in the pool.

"Nice pedicure."

"My girl from the nail salon is coming by the house and giving me manicures and pedicures. She even waxes me. Get this, my hairdresser is coming by and get this, my Botox lady is going to come by as well. I am not going to become some wrinkled up old lady."

"You're beautiful," I say which is true, but I know that it's what she wants to hear.

"Well thank you."

"So, I wanted to ask you. You had asked me if I could just come and stay here."

"Wait, are you offering to come and stay here? The boys will be so excited. They hate me but they love you."

"They do not hate you. But wait. I have a few jobs I do, and I can't quit them all."

"Why not?"

"Because I can't put all my eggs in one basket."

"What does that mean?"

"I need to have a few jobs in the long run, so what if I live here, but once in a while I go out and do another job."

"You need to take the boys with you everywhere you go. Don't leave them with me."

"That's a terrible idea. My car isn't even that safe. Have you seen it?"

"I'll give you a car to drive if you take the boys with you."

"Okay, what if whenever I leave, we try this. I give the boys an assignment to do, and I keep checking in on them while I'm gone. Can we try that?"

"Why can't you take them?"

"I have a client I take to the hospital."

"They can go."

"I have a client I buy weed for."

"Oh my god. Buy me some weed. Buy me some. I want that weed that's 20 percent THC."

"Okay, unless you've been smoking, you'll be catatonic. You have two sons here."

"But you'll be here! You are buying me the weed." She hands me two hundred dollars. "Get me the best they have and come right back here. We have a deal. You get the boys doing whatever you tell them to do and try to keep them going while you're gone. But don't be gone too long because I am going to be higher than God."

"I thought you were working."

"Work is overrated, don't you think? You know when I was first dating, I was terrified of getting AIDS or herpes and when I married Richard and he was a doctor and free of diseases, I thought I had scored. I keep thinking now that maybe we should have had something else in common besides being free of diseases. I mean we live in this house with Thing One and Thing Two and these two monsters are just running up and down the stairs and it hurts my head." It's probably not the time to say that even sunlight is going to hurt your head when you've had that much to drink.

I take off to get the weed and the phone rings. I put in my headphones. It's Ed. "You left without saying goodbye."

"I was kicked out."

"Is that what happened?"

"She's lived with you for years, I'm sure she felt like I was in her place."

"Can you come by tomorrow to run me to the doctor? And I have something for you? Maybe around eleven?"

I want to think that he misses me, but I'm just the driver. When I get back to Sheryl's house with the weed, she starts smoking right away and falls asleep by the pool. The boys and I carry her inside and into the living room. We don't know how many times that spring we will continue that ritual. We make popcorn and watch Star Trek. "Do you think aliens will come to rescue us?" they ask.

"They could take us up in their spaceships," I say, "And take us to another world. Any world would be better than this one."

CHAPTER 14

APRIL 24TH

IN NEW YORK, THE COVID NUMBERS are terrifying. The mass graves on Hart Island for unclaimed bodies, the bodies rotting in the streets, the hospitals overflowing, but here on the West Coast, the virus is chugging away at a slow pace; we are thanking our warm weather, the fact that we are spread out. In other parts of the country, they're blaming New Yorkers for their privilege and for being coastal elites, but I, who have always wanted to live in New York, am watching the whole thing and hoping the best for my dream city. Los Angeles feels like a blond untouched woman out here standing by the ocean. The virus only a whisper. Nobody seems to know anyone who has actually died. We wear masks in public, but everybody has people coming by their houses. We don't have Covid yet.

I'm living at Sheryl's and I've got a nice routine going. I manage to take the boys with me on my cleaning jobs and even when I go to see Ed. He is delighted with them and teaches them all kinds of things about electricity, mathematics, and how roads were built. Why is it that men care how roads were built? You drive on them. He begins with the Romans and tells them that any great civilization builds roads. The boys love the lessons on roads because it leads to a lesson on trucks and why truckers are important to the nation. The boys want to understand trucks and trains.

I'm not sure why this particular crisis has undone Sheryl, but she isn't ready to be left alone with her boys during this time. I try buying her weed that isn't so strong, but she just smokes more of it. She has her girlfriend Candy over and night after night, they drink tequila and smoke and when Candy leaves, she keeps going until she falls asleep, and we carry her to bed. I feel like she's avoiding something.

Ed gave me a book that I'd been reading at his house, called *The Argonauts* by Maggie Nelson. I too am creating my own kind of family, but I love Maggie's queer family so fiercely. When I lived at the cult, we were told that family is what you make of it, but what they meant was that Y was creating a harem that worked for him. Usually when someone says that you don't get the family you want, they mean women and children don't get the family they want. Men walk all over god's world getting whatever they want as far as the eye can see. I wonder about the girls I left behind and what Y is doing to them. When I was alone with Y, he made it clear what he meant to do to me. He made it clear that he owned my body. I'm driving with the boys in the evening to the Santa Monica Pier to see the phosphorescence. We even have a picnic.

We get to the beach, and we find a place to park by someone's house because the actual beach parking is closed off, and I get out our basket and we walk down to the sand. No one is supposed to be going to the beach, but we can see there are a few people there. We spread out a blanket, and the boys eat their sandwiches and run up and down the beach until the darkness rolls in and we see the ocean shining, glowing blue. It's as if there's a blue fire inside those waves just before they hit the shore. The boys get their feet wet, but I watch to make sure they don't get too far out. By this time, there are more people on the beach, a couple of lovers are on the lifeguard station. I'm pretty sure they're having sex, I can hear them murmuring in low sweet Spanish, and around us a thrum of Spanish voices. I'm thinking this is becoming more of a party, someone has music playing, and it floats across the sand, and the thrum of music and laughter feels so joyous like before Covid happened and gathering was a good thing, and then up near my car, I see the flash of blue and red and I collect the picnic basket and in a moment the boys and I are making a run for the car. The cops are clearing the beaches. I wish I could stay and help someone; I am almost certain that someone, perhaps that couple at the lifeguard tower will be arrested, but I am nobody and I have to get these boys back to their house before I get them in trouble and lose my job.

"We're lucky we didn't get thrown in jail," the boys say as we drive away.

What was the chance that was going to happen? I think.

WHEN I ARRIVE AT THE HOUSE, we carry their mother inside, cover her with a blanket, put a pillow under her head and I put the boys to sleep. The next day, while she is sleeping, we go to Chuck and Sally's. I set them up in the living room to do their schoolwork while I clean the house. Sally is angry when I arrive.

"What's up?" I ask. She follows me around the bedroom while I clean, Sophia is back at in the kitchen. Sally sits on the bed.

"I am sick of listening to him," she says.

"Last time I was here you guys were going at it."

"That's it," she says. "That's all we have in common. I don't know how we have made it this far, but I cannot be locked up with him through the election. He keeps telling me his war stories. The way he tells it, you'd think he won the Vietnam War by himself or that he was practically a general. He is always telling stories about what he did in the war. It's as if his life stopped after the war. Afterward he had a whole life; he worked at a company, but he's one of those guys who the most exciting part of his life is the war part."

"You're lucky the best part of his life wasn't high school; that would be worse. I've heard that soldiers who actually fought in wars don't talk about it. Like guys in a locker room who say they slept with eighteen women are probably jacking off in the shower."

"He fought, but I think three things happened and he just repeats those over and over."

"I've noticed," I say, cleaning the bathroom and moving on to making the bed. "I'm thinking that sanity is defined by the gap between one's reality and the reality others have of you. For example, if you think you are sweet, kind generous and attractive but no one else thinks so, that's a reality gap. A lot of men think they are brilliant and important. According to our psych professor, more men have narcissistic personality disorder than women."

"That's all I need is some college student handing out a psych eval," she says.

"The other thing I've noticed is that most people think they are way less patronizing and less racist than they actually are."

Sally laughs, "I'm totally not racist," she says. "I'm fine with blue people."

"You mean cops?"

"No, I mean actual blue people."

"But there are no blue people." I say, "unless you mean aliens."

"I'm fine with anyone. I don't see color. I want them to all have a place. I think everyone should have a chance if they come to this country to learn English and then do their job, pay taxes. Look, I need to go on a vacation, so my friend and I are driving up the coast, so I am going to pay you to not come next week. He won't make that much of a mess. I can't have you coming again when I'm not here. I think he's going to have girls over again."

"You chill? With the girls?" I ask.

"I guess." Sally sighs. "I just need to get through Covid and then I'll decide what to do with my husband who thinks he's a war hero."

"I'm just going to say something. If you say you don't see color, it means you don't see people for who we are. Talking about 'them learning English' is part of the problem. The way I see it, we are all trying to survive on this planet. Some of us got more coins. I don't want to disagree with you."

"But you're going to anyway."

"Well, maybe I should shut up now, but you can stay in this country and not learn English."

"I'm just saying they ought to learn English."

"The word 'they,' is problematic, but this is your house, so I'm going to just state that and be quiet."

"Food for thought. Maybe we should go back to talking about marriage."

"Well, I guess I'm not clear why women need men. Maybe there's something I'm missing."

"Wow, that's giving marriage a bad rap. That's what you see when you go to people's houses?"

"Exactly. These beautiful women making money, running the house, and acting miserable when their husbands show up. The men are bullies. The men say they want to take care of the women. What they want is to run the show their way and to have the women wait on them. Actually, there's one guy who insists on doing the cooking and the laundry, but at that house, you can't even tell his wife lives there. It's like she's been erased. It's all him." Sally's phone rings and she takes Chuck a sandwich and I get through the rest of my cleaning with my headphones on. She's okay, but I don't like talking with customers. Sooner or later, and it's sooner in my case, I'm going to say something I shouldn't and screw everything up.

When Sally pays me, she says, "You know, not all men are like my husband, just saying, if you turn out to like men, you might find one you like. Sophia has a keeper, right?" Sophia smiles.

Our next house cancelled as soon as Covid started, but now they have us coming back. They didn't seem thrilled that four of us would show up, but I explained that the two boys would sit off outside and do their homework. We pull into the gated community of Bell Canyon and up to the big house. Their pool boy/ gardener opens the door. "Glad to see you back," he says. "Place is a pigsty." We walk in and what hits me right away is how bad the smell is. The smell is cat shit, unwashed clothing, rancid food, and cigarettes. How can they stand it? I tell the boys to go around to the patio and get set up and I'll check on them. Mrs. Lionel, our only real celebrity client comes down the stairs. She lives here with her husband and their two cats. Clearly nobody has changed the cat litter, done the dishes or the laundry, and there is filth underfoot. We get to work with a vengeance. We used to clean this house in three hours together; somehow, I don't think she is going to pay us for more than that. I check on the boys, but they are being good, and I am working faster than I had thought possible, and we get the litter out, the house cleaned, the laundry done, beds made, dishes put away, everything done in just over three hours. At the end, I ask her if she needs anyone to make a grocery run. Mrs. Lionel does TV work, and she thinks when she goes to the grocery store everyone recognizes her, although I doubt it. She often pays me to get her groceries. I have no idea how she's been eating but from the look of things, a lot of pizza. She looks a little heavy too. Also, a lot of wine bottles.

"I've got a list," she says. "Also, my daughter is moving in with her kids next week, so we'll need you to look after them as well. You can bring these boys along too, but I'll need you to tutor my grandchildren. You tutor, right?"

"Yeah," I say, "but I charge for that."

"No problem, what do you charge?"

"Thirty dollars an hour.," I say. I've never made that much in my life, but it sounds good.

"Good, bring the boys along, we'll have a little classroom." It crosses my mind once that if the boy's father, who is a doctor, knew that they were going to be in a little Covid classroom somewhere, he'd be surprised, but life is full of little surprises and he's at the hospital, and I am here making decisions for his stoner wife.

When I get back to the house, Sheryl and Candy are swimming in the pool. "Come and join us, my little angels," she says. "I love you." She has that blurry red eyed glassy look. Her hair is a jumble. Some days I'll think, how long can this go on? But then, I'll think, I am sleeping indoors. The boys are finishing school, I am finishing school. She's enjoying Covid. My Venmo transactions are clearing, I almost have enough to start UCLA in January. What is the problem? "Let's have ice cream." She says. "Mia, go get us some ice cream. Don't you work here?"

I set down my stuff and get the boys their favorite, chocolate chip cookie dough and some cones and bring it all outside. "What's your favorite, ma'am?" I ask.

"Don't ma'am me," she says. "We're practically the same age." This is in fact, not true, but it is my finding, that you spend Botox to make yourself look younger, and then sometimes you slice off fifteen years. "I want the strawberry cheesecake." I get her ice cream and ask Candy. Candy tends to have a drink of tequila and then switch to soda water.

"I'm fine," she says. "I'll help you take the stuff inside."

"Don't leave me," Sheryl says, "She can get it. She's the help." The boys both jump in to help as well, and Sheryl is left alone bobbing on the side of the pool with her ice cream.

"Sheryl seems crazy," one of the boys says, and I turn. I realize they've stopped calling her Mom, or Mama. "She is a crazy," the other says.

"She's your mother," I say. "Why don't you finish your cones outside?"

Candy turns to me. "When should we get in touch with Richard?" she says.

"He's coming home soon," I say.

"Look what I found," Sheryl says. She pulls out an M80. "We're going to set this off right here in our backyard and it is going to be a great firework explosion."

"Where did you find that?" I say.

"Richard had it hidden," she says, "but he isn't here, and we are going to have fun without him." The M80 is sitting beside her. She had it in a bag and has clearly just remembered it in her haze. "We are doing this now," she says.

"Let me talk to the boys a minute," I say. "Come on boys." They don't want to leave now that they see the firework, but they follow me inside. "Boys," I say. "I'm going to make this clear to you. Because of fires, fireworks are illegal. Secondly your mother is stoned and shouldn't be doing this. I am going to take away that M80 and hide it so she can't find it. Are we clear?" They nod.

When I go out to take away the M80 from Sheryl, she is still surprisingly wide awake.

"When are we doing this firework?"

"Not tonight. The boys have gone to bed, so I'd like to put this away."

"You put this away, you're fired. Get out of here tonight. I'll leave your money on the table."

"Okay," I say. I take the M80. She's drunk enough that she doesn't follow me. I hide it in the garage and then I come back to say goodbye to the boys.

"Can we call you in the morning if she changes her mind?"

"You know my number. You have your dad's number too if things go wrong here."

"We aren't allowed to call our dad unless there's an emergency."

"You're getting pretty close to an emergency," I say. As I'm driving away, I feel oddly light-headed. I haven't walked away from any well-paying jobs before. But in California, fires are serious, and fireworks cause fires. I want to be part of the good in the world in a small way. I want to believe that the universe will take care of me.

I sleep in my car, glad to be back in Topanga, do a weed run in the morning, and around eleven, I get a call from her. "Where are you?"

"You fired me last night," I say.

"Why did I do that? Were you mouthing off something awful?"

"I guess I was," I say, "But I apologize."

"Well get your ass back here and get me some gummies."

"I've got some in the car."

That night I bring the boys with me when I go to Sophia's house, I bring a lot of food because it's my birthday and I know they are going to roll out a cake. It's such an odd thing for me to watch these twins experiencing the only normal family part of their life in the El Salvadoran household of my friends. Everyone speaks in a mix of Spanish and English. We always have pupusas and whatever they cook up with stuff I bring over but there is always rice, and for the boys the great thing is the salsa music, the stories of the crossing and the stories of the days of hard work, the joy and love; it's everything that makes up a first-generation American family. Crowded into one room; there is no place in that one-bedroom apartment that does not smell like Latin food and in which you do not hear music and do not feel loved. It's not the promised land they hoped for. When they arrived in Van Nuys, every sign in Spanish, El Salvadoran restaurants everywhere, they must have thought this was some extension of home. On the way home, the boys beg to listen to Spanish music. We pull into the driveway to the flash of red and blue police cars.

"Stay in the car boys," I say. Richard comes toward me.

"Do you have my boys?"

"Yes, I'm their babysitter. Why are the police here?"

"I came home for the weekend to find my wife passed out, my kids gone, and I didn't know there was a babysitter, I had made it clear there was not to be a babysitter. How long have you been here?" I stare at him. "Okay, I'm going to tell the cops to go, and you and I are going to have a come to Jesus moment. Boys off to bed. You go sit in the living room." The only reason I don't just drive away right now is that I have not been paid. I'm thinking, *Screw this.*

He comes into the living room. "Talk," he says.

"Call Candy," I say.

"Okay, but I want to hear from you."

"I want you to hear from Candy first."

"Okay," he taps the keys and goes into the other room. I can hear his voice rising and falling and then after about ten minutes he returns. "I think I got it," he says. "But let's hear your side of this."

"I think being a mother is challenging for your wife. Maybe girls would have been easier. When you left her alone, she caved in and decided to just medicate while you were gone, and she called me because she was a responsible enough parent to know someone should take care of the kids. I have gotten through their schoolwork which they were not doing and taken them to the beach, and tonight we went to see friends who by the way all tested negative, and the boys have been tested negative."

"Good for you, I think I can take it from here. How much do we owe you?"

I write down how much it is and hand it to him and he takes the money out of his wallet. "One more thing. Your M80 is in the garage above the tools. You have to climb on a ladder to get it. You'll see it. She was going to light it with the boys." He hands me another twenty.

"Jesus," he says. "I've been saving people's lives. I called a few times, and I guess she seemed okay, I didn't get that everything was falling apart."

"Can I say goodnight to the boys?"

"Sure," he says.

"Sing that song to us," they say. "The one about hands."

"The one my friend Tallulah taught me?" I ask.

"Yeah, that one."

"It's an old song," I say, "And you know when Marian Anderson wanted to sing this song, the white people didn't want to allow her to sing it at Constitution Hall."

"That wouldn't happen now though," they say.

"You'd be surprised what happens now," I say, and I sing, "He's got the whole world in his hands. He's got you and me brother in his hands. He's got the whole world in his hands." I drive back to Topanga. I think of those boys in their safe protected home. The police are never coming for them. My fellow students who are of color tell me how their parents tell them to be careful around cops when they're eight. Don't grab your phone or your wallet. Hands up. Do these boys need to worry like those kids at the beach, like my fellow students, like Tallulah's brother who got arrested driving down the Five with her and her baby in the back seat? What kind of civilization encourages crushing defenseless people? The police force, the justice system, the student loan system, Wall Street, all of it is rigged against us, those of us who are poor, of color, queer. I don't know if voting in one old white man will help but I certainly want to get rid of this old white man whose hanging out at 1600 Pennsylvania Avenue and spending his days golfing, Tweeting; his life one big game of Go Fish for more money, more applause for me, me, me. I drive down to the water. I want to wake up next to the heaving sounds of the Pacific Ocean. We at the bottom have our simple pleasures. For me, the ocean is one of them.

CHAPTER 15

APRIL 26TH

WHEN I WAKE UP BY THE ocean, I search my car for the piece of leftover carrot cake from my birthday and I have it for breakfast; it tastes like joy. It's Sunday, so maybe no one will need me today. I take a long walk on the beach and see gulls fighting each other for bits of dead fish. I'm nearly finished with my schoolwork. When I finish my walk, I read Lauren Groff. I've decided to spend another night by the beach. There's no reason to be anywhere until tomorrow.

I keep thinking about the twins. Their life has a direction. All these kids who I tutor; all they have to do is stay on the glass elevator. Go to private school. Go to private college. Marry the right person. Get a job at the right accounting firm, tech firm, law firm, or investment firm and you're set. Everything has been laid out for you. Everything has been decided. From pod to butterfly. The big surprise of your life is *which* big law firm, *which* investment banking firm. New York or Los Angeles or San Francisco, possibly Chicago; Goldman Sachs or the Capital Group. According to our econ professor, the rich keep getting richer and passing on wealth and giving each other jobs. They go to Ivy League schools; the men make sure the other men are members of the right clubs; they pass around the wealth and the ability to get wealth. We are the invisible hands and now I see with Covid, we are more necessary and more invisible.

Sophia calls to tell me that her brother who works in a kitchen downtown has Covid and is on a ventilator. They hadn't seen him, but they think he got it at the restaurant. I tell her I'm sure that he'll be okay. By now we know others who've had it. They all recovered. They couldn't smell for days. Her friend Carmen had it by far the worst, but she recovered. Carmen says of any flu she's ever had, Covid is the strangest. You don't just feel like vomiting, you feel like your lungs are being scraped out and not being able to taste and smell feels like some alien is messing with your insides. Carmen said, she felt like something was crawling around inside her body trying to kill her. She said, a cockroach was crawling inside her. She explains this rapidly in Spanish at one of our Saturday gatherings. Somehow the word, "cucaracha," sounds so much creepier in Spanish. I wish I were rich so I could buy us all a little pink house so we could be okay, but the best I can do is buy Saturday dinners and make sure we have enough rice.

All Sunday, I walk on the beach and read in my car. In my classes at Pierce, I meet kids who moved to Los Angeles to become surfers, not realizing that the ocean is cold. They saw movies of all that raw sunshine, and they thought it was warm. It's screamingly cold, and it never gets warm. Whales like it, but let's face it, whales have more blubber than we do. Everything about Los Angeles is a myth. Yes, the girls are beautiful but they're all better than you. Yes, the houses are big, but you can't afford to buy them. The ocean is an hour from almost anywhere you live in Los Angeles, and you have to pay to park near it and it's dirty and too cold to swim in. The tall king palm trees you see in all the movies were brought from Australia.

My schedule has been shifting lately, so I put everything into my Google calendar, but Monday morning Mrs. Royal calls. She wants to know if I can come back and clean the house and she says that she and Mr. Royal are back in town. Can I be there today? I look at my schedule which is getting pretty full. "Would tomorrow work?"

"Yes. But just you."

When I arrive the next day, the Royals are having breakfast. "Sit down," Mr. Royal says. There is no sign of Nick. "Tell us about yourself."

"I go to college at Pierce, and I plan to transfer to UCLA in January. I tutor kids and clean houses."

"What is Sophia hoping for with the child?"

"I don't know. Has she asked for anything?"

"No, we wanted to ask you if she needed anything for the baby."

"Why don't you ask her?"

"We don't want this to get ugly. If she asks for a paternity test, we will have her and her family and her brother deported."

I take out a pen and paper and write it down and read it out loud. "If she asks for a paternity test, you will have her and her family and her brother thrown out of the country, so she better not ask for a test or for anything else? Have I got this?"

"Correct," they both say.

"Understood," I say, and I get up to leave.

"Aren't you going to clean the house?" Mrs. Royal says.

"You know," I say, "On the one hand, I need all the work I can get, because as that baby's godmother, I am paying for half his expenses since his father's family won't pay them, but on the other hand, you just threatened my godson's family and now you want to know if I'm feeling up to getting on my knees and cleaning your toilets?"

"Listen here," Mr. Royal says. "I can find another little person to clean my house whenever I want to. I do more good in the world than you ever will."

"What do you do? Because I help people."

He sighs. "You clean up after people for cash, that's nice. You clean up messes. You're the janitor. I am the CFO of a large company, and I give money to charities, and I helped the current president get elected. I'm taking care of keeping things in order."

I stand up. "Sir," I say, "you're probably right. I'm sure you know much more than I do. I'm tired."

"Oh yes," he says. "You are tired of your parents paying for you to go to college and paying for your fancy cars and apartments while you get to bitch about everything. What would your parents think of your walking away from a job working for a CFO like me?"

"I don't know," I say. "My parents threw me out a long time ago."

Mrs. Royal follows me out to the car.

"Are you coming back?" she says, "because Sophia doesn't answer her phone."

"Look, Sophia is the grandmother of your son's baby. You are the grandmother also, so no, don't expect to see Sophia. Your husband is a liar when he says my parents are taking care of me. I've only met my father once. If I were being taken care of by my parents, they would be paying for my apartment and sending me to college, but I'm living in my car."

"What if I call you when he's out of town and pay you double so you can give Sophia money for the baby. Honestly, I can't find another housekeeper during Covid. I do trust you."

"I'm only saying yes because Juan needs health insurance, and they are really tight now."

"He's a beautiful baby. I want to see him again."

"Mrs. Royal, I think you should be careful." She hands me an envelope.

"This is for Juan," she says. "I want to see him again. Nick is at rehab and he's a bad kid. Juan might be our family's only hope."

"I'm sure Mr. Royal will be pleased you see it that way. Be safe. Call me when he's gone."

I DRIVE TO MRS. LIONEL'S HOUSE just as her daughter arrives with the two grandchildren. "Ah, Mia, you are just in time, you can give the kids some Spanish lessons while we unpack."

"We don't want to learn Spanish," one of the girls says. "We want to play video games. We hate school. School is stupid. We want ice cream."

"Girls," I say, "come with me." The girls follow me outside. "Now," I say, "I've been made the boss of you. And," I say in my vampire voice, "if you do not do as I say, I will suck your blood." They sit down. "We are going to learn Spanish, and then the good news is that we all swim in the pool and have lunch. I will time our Spanish lesson and make sure it is fun and under an hour. Are we good?" I have my kid management skills down with the boys, and I know I can manage these two. Sophia is cleaning the house, but she comes out to see how the Spanish lessons are going.

"I can teach this," she laughs. "*Estrella* means star, I know that."

It's not lost on me that it is ridiculous that I am giving Spanish lessons while Sophia cleans the house. All I can think is that it's a good thing we are friends. Whenever we've joked about her giving lessons to kids, she's made clear that teaching is not her skill set, she likes listening to her music and getting through the house, but still, I think, in another world, she could be teaching. I spend too much time thinking of the unfairness of the world.

The girls are listening to their Spanish phonetics recordings, and I pull Sophia aside.

"I got $500 for Juan," I say. "From the Royals, after they insulted me quite a bit, then she gave over this money for him. She wants to see him again."

"That's not good," she says. "I don't trust them."

"Me neither," I say. "But let's take the money and get some diapers and clothes for him."

CHAPTER 16

MAY 1ST

AFTER I FINISH TUTORING, I HELP Sophia with the house. When we finish, she's meeting Roberto at the hospital to visit her brother. He's been on a ventilator now for weeks, and so far nothing is working. She and her brother came together during the twelve-year war in El Salvador with their mother, who then went back to stay with their other twelve siblings who survived childbirth. Two of them were killed in the war. I can't imagine how that woman gave birth to fourteen children. I met her when she came to stay with them for a few months, such a beautiful old face, she had seen so much history. She moved into Sophia's kitchen and started making tortillas, and we said, "Can you make them with your eyes closed?" and she just closed her eyes and they kept coming out perfectly round one on top of one another. I can't go to the hospital even though I know her brother because I'm not a relative, so I wait outside. I'm so tired of everything. Sophia comes back, crying and Roberto asks me to spend the night and stay with her. I spend the night sleeping with her. He sleeps with the kids, so I'm there when the call comes from the hospital and her brother, Enrique Jimenez is dead.

We arrive at the hospital. They want to know what funeral home we want his body shipped to. Sophia is wailing and Roberto is holding her. I tell him to give me a minute and I go in the hallway and google "cheap cremation." What comes up is "affordable cremation." I realize that sounds better. There's one in Mission Hills, and I'm sure they speak Spanish there, so I say that's our place of choice. When we arrive, there's a man in a suit who tells us right away that for $2500 we will be informed of the very moment our loved one is being cremated and then we will have a presidential urn in which to keep our loved one's ashes. I step up and say to the man in the suit, "Can I see you for a moment?"

In the next room, I say, "We have no money, so get someone who speaks Spanish to go back in there and offer your least expensive option."

"Look," he says, "you'll be practically walking out of here with your loved one's ashes in a box."

"We can take our loved one's ashes to the ocean." I say.

"That's illegal unless you are three nautical miles from land," he says, "but I hear you. We have an option for under seven hundred dollars. I have someone who speaks Spanish." I want to get out of this suffocating little place for under a grand. It's insulting to me that this guy is trying to scam us. I pay for the cremation and Roberto takes Sophia to the car.

When someone dies of Covid, you don't gather, and we aren't a Zoom kind of family. Roberto is on the phone for days, and I fill in for Sophia's jobs, but finally, she seems to want work to fill in her pain. Their family isn't going to be able to pay bills unless she's working. Olivia is taking care of Juan and he needs diapers and food.

It's been a few days and I keep wondering how long before I'll hear from Sheryl, and then I do. "Hey, Mia, Richard's gone back to work."

"Good for him," I say.

"Could you come by with some edibles?" she says. I pause. "Usual delivery fee?"

"Okay, later this afternoon," I say.

As I'm driving out, I think about the fact that I've ended up with clients who treat me pretty nicely. Almost like I'm a person. The boys rush out to the car. "Did you have a good time with your dad?" I ask.

"Yes, but we missed you, and now he's gone, and we want you back," they say in unison.

"Well, I don't know if your mom wants me to hang out," I say.

"Sheryl said you can stay as long as you want," they say.

"Did she now?"

Sheryl is sitting at the dining room table at work. "Good to see you," she says. "Could you sit down?" I sit and she gets me a glass of ginger beer. Weird that she noticed I often have ginger beer with me. "I'm not going to do the edibles until later in the day. I'm working and I'm supervising the boys, but I would like a break and Richard agrees that having a break now and then is a good idea. I hope you could use some more work and the boys miss you," she says. Clearly, she has rehearsed this several times.

Her phone rings, and she gets up to answer.

I'm left alone. The boys peek in and I wave for them to leave but I wish I had someone to call and talk this over. She comes back covering the phone, "This is going to be a few minutes," she says. *Great*, I think, *I do have time. Who should I call?*

I call Sally and explain the situation. "She's kind of mean to me. She looks down on me. She thinks I'm little people, but it's money."

"The ubiquitous cruelty of the upper classes," she says.

"The what?" I ask.

"You've broken the pattern by being gone. Set a new pattern with her. She doesn't have to be nice to you. She just has to pretend. Most rich people pretend to be nice to the people around them because they have no respect for the people who work for them. Tell her she needs to pretend. You can't see what's in her heart, but you can ask for civility and respect. Which is what we lost with this president."

"Wait," I say. "I thought you were hovered around Fox News because you loved the president."

"Shut up," she says, "I tolerate my own husband by watching Fox News. Do what I say, not what I do. Go stand up for yourself. And by the way, don't be a baby. I know it's nice when people are nice to you, but it's not a god given right."

I finish my ginger beer and Sheryl returns. "I've got a request," I say. "If I were in your factory making boots for you and you were walking through screaming at me, I would have on headphones and I would be thinking, well, you can imagine, but some cuss words, because I wouldn't like you.

I'm in your home taking care of your children while you are insulting me and treating me rudely and talking down to me. I'd like to request that you treat me like a human being, just pretend while I'm here that I matter and deserve respect. As soon as I leave you can start talking smack about me, but hopefully not in front of the boys."

"I get it," Sheryl says. "I really do. People can change. I really wasn't at my best, but I'm going to turn it around."

"I'm just curious," I say. "I get the Ivy Leaguers who look down on everyone. Who are you looking down on?"

I see the effort it must take to pull herself together. Her hair is curled; her makeup applied. Her lipstick is on. Her earrings are in place. "You don't understand what makes a person crazy. What pissed me off was having everything. I never thought my life would turn sour. The handsome, adoring doctor husband is never there. My sons despise me, and they adore you. You're just a nobody. I wanted magic. What did you think your life would be?"

"Well, I was hoping they would stop beating me long enough that I could run away and go to school and now I'm just hoping to finish college. The boys want to swim."

The sunset is pouring across the pool when we dive in; she keeps it heated year-round. What a thing to live this life and not even appreciate it. The boys are enraptured to see me and want to know when I'll be back. The sun threads gold through the palm trees. Los Angeles is so beautiful that when it shines on you, you almost believe that you are shining as well.

THE DAY WE GOT ENRIQUE'S ASHES, the sunlight was beautiful. It was a perfect California day. We drove with his ashes down to the beach where he liked to play volleyball, and we sat there and drank beer and told stories and the sunlight poured along the beach and for Sophia's sake, we couldn't take the ashes back to their tiny apartment, so we drove up the coast and dropped in on Sophia's aunt who has a one-bedroom house in Santa Barbara, and she buried the ashes in her garden. She's been living on such a tiny amount of fixed income for so long, I don't know how she keeps that little place. She promised to plant flowers for him. In all your saddest moments, in all your loneliest times, the California sky will respond with sunshine and blue air. You will be despondent, beaten up, sitting next to your junkie brother, or your beloved friend who's just lost her brother, and the California sky will respond unflinchingly with sunshine.

CHAPTER 17

―――

MAY 5TH

I'VE LIVED IN MY CAR FOR a year now, and what I know
about summer is that it gets hot. It's too hot to stay in the
Valley where it can be 115 degrees. Some un-housed people
do it, and they get used to it, but some of them die in the
heat as well and their bodies are found. Usually, I move to
the beach where it's cooler by about twenty degrees. I wake
on Thursday and look at my calendar. It's my day to drive Ed
to the doctor, then I'm going to tutor the girls for a couple
hours, and then see the twins in the late afternoon. I feel a
little weird. Like everyone, I have phantom Covid symptoms
pretty often. Whenever I feel the least bit sick, I'll check to
see how my sense of smell is going. I feel my throat; definitely
something is wrong. I feel my chest, yes, something is wrong.
But then, maybe I'm imagining it. I've been sleeping in a car,
so I'm not exactly comfortable. I get out and stretch. I feel
better.

By the time I've gotten coffee, I've convinced myself that
I'm fine. I'm ready to work. When I get to Ed's, he says he's

not feeling well and he needs me to take him into the hospital in his wheelchair. I just saw him yesterday when I was dropping off groceries and I helped him try on some clothes. He doesn't look like himself. But he says he doesn't have Covid symptoms. "I can smell my coffee," he says. "So, I'm pretty sure, I don't have it."

"Neither do I," I say.

"Anything wrong with you?"

"I felt weird this morning," I say, "but I'm sure it's nothing, my body is just lazy sometimes."

"Your body is not lazy."

I park his car in the handicapped area and get him into the chair and wheel him into Cedars. "I need her with me," he says.

"We'll need to check both of your temperatures," the nurse says holding up a thermometer. "We can take the chair from here."

"I need her with me," Ed says again. I'm surprised. Maybe he's losing it a bit, but this is Cedars, and they come over to take my temperature and his.

"You both have a temperature," the man says. "We need to test you for Covid." We are taken to a room and immediately isolated as if we have Ebola and they come back in forty-five minutes to say we are negative, but they want a urine sample. An hour later, Ed's doctor enters the room.

"You have pneumonia, Ed," he says, "and so does your assistant. I'm going to guess you've had it for several days."

"Which means I gave it to you," Ed says. "I knew I was feeling bad yesterday."

"Just a moment," the doctor says. "I'll be right back, let me get someone to get you all checked in."

When he comes back, I get to my feet.

"Are you going to keep him overnight?"

"We are going to keep him at least one night and get him going on antibiotics. What about you?"

"I don't have health insurance; don't worry about me. You'll take care of him from here? Are you okay, Ed?" I look over at him, but with the wait, he's fallen asleep. I slip out the door and take his car back to his house. Sitting in my car, I google "walking pneumonia." It's contagious until you've been taking antibiotics for forty-eight hours. I call Mrs. Lionel and Sheryl and let them know that I need to take a couple days off. I google antibiotics online. I can buy some, but it will take a week and they might be bad drugs. Plus, there's the matter of having them shipped to my post office box. I can drive to Tijuana, but that might be unsafe. I've heard of people getting bad drugs there and what if I get sicker? I feel a little wobbly and the idea of driving six hours to Mexico and back does not sound good. Tijuana can be dangerous if you don't know what you're doing. I can go to a clinic, but that would cost a couple hundred. I call Sophia. She knows somebody who will sell me antibiotics for fifty dollars. She has the guy text me. I tell him I want 500 milligrams a day of Levaquin for ten days and he has me meet him in Balboa Park. He's a handsome Mexican guy with a backpack and cool sunglasses. I wish I were meeting him under different circumstances so I could flirt a bit, but it seems a bit crazy to try to get sexy when you have walking pneumonia. I don't ask questions, just lay the cash on the bench and try to make no contact. As soon as I take the medicine, I can feel it working. Since I have a couple days vacay, I finish my schoolwork and turn in everything. I'm getting As in all my classes, but most people are during Covid. The professors are just handing out the As like M&Ms.

I'm worried about seeing anybody at all, so I'm going to have to just eat what I have in my car which is two cans of tuna and my Gatorade. I fall asleep and wake up twelve hours later, drink more Gatorade, take another walk and now I'm hungry. I call Ed and he says they are keeping him one more day and then I need to come get him. On Saturday, I go to pick him up, and I'm excited to have real food. "Where did you go?" he asks as soon as we get in the car.

"I just took off. Your doctor said he was taking care of you."

"He said you had pneumonia as well," he says.

"I've been on antibiotics."

"Drive me to where you stay," he says.

"It doesn't matter," I say.

"Just drive." We drive to Diana's property on Topanga and I say, "Here we are."

"Take me to the main house," he says. "I know this woman." I drive up the hill and he says, "Just stay in the car," and he knocks on the door. Diana and her wolf appear. She sees me and she comes out and sits. They sit several feet apart and take off their masks. I'm sitting in the car listening to my Pandora play Nina Simone and I feel like a child being discussed by their parents—only these aren't my parents.

"Love me," she sings. And I think that's all I want is for someone to love me. To cherish me. Because if they did, I could breathe. I could figure things out. I don't have to be rich. I don't need stuff. I just want an alive green womb place. I just want to keep the wolves from the door. I want to stop eating cruelty for breakfast. Diana goes inside and gets a bowl for each of them, it looks like olives. Diana, before Covid used to travel to Africa and talk with elephants. I know this because I've looked her up online. I've never seen elephants except in the zoo. Most people haven't seen wild elephants unless they're rich enough to go on safari. Ed calls me over.

"I'd like to invite you," Diana says, "to stay in the yurt on my property. There's a locker in the yurt where you can keep your stuff safely. There's a bed, a small fridge, and a kitchen. I think it's time you had a home. By the way, I appreciate your getting my groceries and medical supplies."

"No problem," I say. "Thank you. I can't thank you enough. This is really so nice of you. You won't regret it. I'm happy to keep getting your supplies," I say trying to sound helpful.

She puts her hands over my head. "Blessings upon you," she says. "Blessings on your life, on your breath, on your coming and on your going." She and the wolf disappear, and Ed and I go to check out the yurt. It's a cool little dome shaped house with a small fridge, a tiny hot plate, a beautiful queen-sized bed with a comforter, and a closet thing.

"What is this?" I say.

"It's an armoire," he says. "For your clothes. Do you have any?"

"No," I say, "but it's nice to think I have a place for future clothes. Wow, this is my own little home, and I have you to thank for this. How do you know her?"

"I'm part of her cabal," he says.

"Really, is she part of some secretive group?"

"It's called Dare," he says, "don't worry, it's not political unless you count saving the world."

"I want to save the world," I say. "Like Batman."

"Why don't you let me sit outside while you get settled here."

It doesn't take long to unpack and then I invite Ed in to see. I even found some flowers and a vase. I've put my books on the bookcase and they look good. "Okay," he says. "Two things, Diana says we have to burn sage to dedicate this place, so she gave me this." He takes out a bundle of white sage.

"You think the sage burning is cool?" I ask. "I've heard that it's cultural appropriation to burn sage."

"I think we're okay," he says. "Diana grew this herself to bless her own property, and we aren't going to steal any Native American smudging rituals, okay? Usually you have to do the corners of the house. But this little yurt has no corners."

"Okay," he lights it and I say, "May this house be blessed."

He says, "May this house be safe."

"Gratitude," I say.

"Live long and prosper," he says.

"How did you know I was a Trekkie?" I say and he laughs.

"One more thing." He takes out a bottle of mezcal and a couple of shot glasses. "This is called 'Mezcales de Leyenda.'" He pours us each a small bit and we raise our glasses.

"To life, to home," he says.

"To home," I say, and we both take a taste. The stuff is good. If sex turns out to be as good as mezcal, I'll wish I hadn't waited so long. This stuff could keep you warm at night. I'm sitting on the bed, and he's sitting on the one chair. He puts the bottle on the shelf for me to keep.

"No college boyfriend?" he asks.

"The thing is," I say. "I've stayed away from boyfriends and drugs and alcohol for the most part. I've had beer although I don't go to parties. I stay away from beer pong. That can get crazy. You can end up drinking a lot of beer, which I would do, because I know I wouldn't be good at the pong. I'm not going to let go and relax around anyone. The reason is that one misstep, and it's over for me. There is no safety net. I have this friend who is more of an acquaintance in my history class, we've been texting since Covid; in fact I had coffee with her once. Her name is Tallulah. She had a brother and when I met her, she introduced me to one of his friends. I liked him, we hung out a bit, but I realized that I couldn't really date him, I was just afraid that if I started to like him and we got involved, then I wouldn't be able to save him or myself or anyone if things went wrong. Tallulah's brother got picked up by the cops for nothing."

"You don't get picked up by the cops for nothing."

"You do if you're Black."

"You have to break the law." I'm having such a good time here, and I don't want to break the spell. I stop.

"Finish your story," he says.

"He was stopped for driving a red Plymouth Barracuda."

"I don't understand why they drive vehicles that will make them get stopped."

"I don't want to disagree with you because you are being my friend. And I don't have a whole lot of friends. But it is my opinion that if you want to drive a red car, you should be able to. I'm not saying that girls are smart when they to go to parties and get drunk and dress slutty. That's another conversation that we had in the feminism classes and that's for another glass of mescal. But, for African Americans, I'm just saying, if I were a cool African American guy, I might not want to drive a Prius or a Toyota van. I might drive a cool car. And I might think I shouldn't get stopped. Does that make sense?"

"It does. And I like that you care. You're a good person. I might be learning from you. To not be such an asshole."

"You just found me a yurt."

"So what happened to her brother?"

"He was thrown in jail for the night because he talked smack to the police officers and then it was a holiday weekend, so they kept him for days, and Tallulah sold some drugs to get him out of jail and it's a long story, but her parents had to step in and she ended up not getting a felony, but that scared the shit out of me. That whole chain of events. Because if you love someone you start doing stupid shit for them."

"Like you do for Sophia's family."

"Yeah, I'm in with them. They're my family; we help each other."

"But you're all struggling together."

"That's why we're trying not to screw up. We're not selling drugs or doing drugs or breaking the law."

"What do you see as your future?"

"Did I ever tell you about the Church of Y?" I ask.

"No,"

"Let me drive you home, and I'll tell you on the way." I'm worried he'll get bored.

"In the Church of Y, they beat kids a lot, and the whole time I was there, I just wanted to leave. And since I got away, I've just thought of survival. Even though I'm going to college, that's just because it's a thing to do when you have no work skills. Give me a few months in this little place. I'll come up with a plan. I'm climbing Maslow's hierarchy of needs."

"Let's stop at the store on the way home," he says. "We're buying you groceries."

"Thank you so much," I say. "Why so altruistic?"

"Why the big vocabulary?"

"The vocab?" I say, "I'm reading up a storm. I'm going to be one of those smarty pants people who's unbearable. I am in college, you know. I'm taking classes in anthropology."

"You have a long way to go," he says. That night, I put avocados, mangos, peaches, and granola bars in a basket on my little table. I see that Diana has left me a gift outside wrapped up. I take it inside and unwrap it. It's a cloud painting to put on the wall above my bed and a journal. My first piece of art. I can look up at the cloud painting when I wake. It's a huge sky, with clouds and the sun behind them. I like thinking about that sun behind them. I write in the journal about this new beginning of my life.

When I wake, I make myself instant coffee and step outside on the balcony of the yurt. Right outside my door, there's a mother deer and a fawn. I stand still. The mother deer slowly moves off with the fawn up the hill, and I see other deer eating grass. I sit down on the steps of the yurt and start crying although I'm not sure why. I'm crying for my mother and for the deer and for Juan and for all the unloved moments of my life and I'm thinking of Tallulah and how telling that story makes my own life feel easy.

"Look at me," I think, "someone just gave me a home. I might be poor, but I'm safe." When I fall asleep in my car, the police are not going to come and shoot me like they did Tyisha Miller. I can go to sleep and wake up. When I see cops, I feel angry for other people, but not for myself. I feel angry, I want a revolution. In my history class, we have been reading Edward Said and Cornel West. Said says that the founders of every empire say they're going to be the good ones; they're not going to plunder and control. They're doing to educate and liberate. But they don't. From the Romans onward to the Americas. The plundering continues. Our professor said that's what every Congress says, that's what every president says, but they all give tax breaks to the rich; they tax the poor, they grind the rest of us into the dirt and we just watch television and let it happen, go Dodgers. Those of us at the very bottom have no voice at all. Our teacher says a revolution is coming. I'm ready for that revolution.

CHAPTER 18

MAY 25TH

I CLEAN MRS. ROYAL'S HOUSE IN the morning, and then I go to Sheryl's with the groceries. She's doing better now; she's usually working when I arrive and the boys are doing homework and have their beds made, but I take over so she can have some time to herself. I can't get used to the masks on everyone. When you go to the market, everyone has their masks, and when you go the bank, it's the oddest thing to see people in masks walking up to the teller and asking for money. It's like a bad movie about the future except it's the present. When I get to Sheryl, she's watching the television which she doesn't do much during the day.

"Come here," she says, "this woman, Fiona Cooper, just posted this video to her Twitter feed. She lives here in LA. I've met her. I don't know her, but I've met her and she's cool and I follow her. I think I'm going to be sick." I walk around to see what she's seeing, and she starts it over from the beginning. Amy Cooper, no relation to Fiona Cooper, is with her dog in Central Park. It takes me a minute to realize it's a cell phone video and I can hear a man's voice speaking calmly, like Gandhi inviting this woman to call the police, and I'm thinking, the police could kill him. They will kill him, and I realize, this is happening. We watch it again and again. Somehow, we're frozen by it. "I thought," she says, "that the people in New York were so much better than us. So much more woke. We struggle out here to figure it all out. But New Yorkers. They know it. But listen to her say 'African American.' Not Black. She's too educated for that. She lives somewhere fancy. She goes to good restaurants. She went to college somewhere nice. She's who we all wish we were if we had clever money. But she's a racist. She could be wearing a hood. The police force is the noose she is dangling for that man. The man is Fiona Cooper's brother."

"You get it," I say. "I was talking with Ed, and he said that the police don't stop Black people unless there's a reason."

"Oh Jesus, that's not true. I'm sure Sophia's husband gets stopped a lot more than my husband. And Black men are in danger every moment of their lives from the police in this country. I do know that. It's a fact in every city. It makes me angry."

My phone rings and it's Tallulah. We've been texting, but she hasn't called me since Covid. "Can I get this," I say. "I need to." She waves to go ahead. "Tallulah," I say. "It's so good to hear from you." I go outside. I can see Sheryl watching and re-watching the video. "What's up?"

"I just wanted to make sure you're okay. I know you were having it rough, and my family's been having such a hard time, I feel so bad I haven't called."

"Hey, you've been texting, I should have called. How are you guys now?"

"My dad died of the coronavirus. He was a butcher, and he had some heart problems. So now it's just me and my mom. We both got it, but we got better. We're going to have a service, and I was kind of hoping you could come."

"Definitely," I say.

"It's not going to be for a while, my mom's still pretty messed up. She hasn't gone to work and it's been two weeks. But the reason I was calling you today was first of all to apologize for not calling you. It's just Covid happened and then my dad. But this Amy Cooper thing has me very angry. I want to come see you. And I kind of need to get out of the house. My aunt is coming over to hang with my mom and I need to get out of here. Any chance I can meet you anywhere?"

"Give me a second," I say. I go in to see Sheryl. "Can my friend Tallulah come over. She wants to talk about this Amy Cooper video."

"Sure, we can talk in the backyard."

"Come ahead," I say.

Tallulah shows up an hour later with fresh strawberries from the Farmer's Market and we all watch the video again. Tallulah begins to talk, and Sheryl and I just listen. Her experience of rage with the video is different than ours. We are outraged. Her rage comes from some deep place inside her. She thinks of Amy Cooper's phone call to the police as attempted murder. Tallulah's voice is melodic explaining the intricacies of oppression from police to the justice system and what she thinks would be required to change it, and she calls her mom and tells her she's spending the night, and I decide to spend the night as well. Somehow the three of us can't stop talking. We're trying to come to some conclusion, but we feel like America is unravelling around us, and the coronavirus is part of it. All of us locked in our homes so long that we've given into madness. I think of what they call "cabin fever," of ships going to mutiny, but this is three hundred million people locked in their homes with a deranged narcissist, a mad Ahab at the helm who keeps reminding us, his TV numbers are incredibly huge, and the numbers we see are the many Americans dying, being buried in unmarked graves. This president doesn't care about the poor, or those of us who are of color. He thinks if we decided to join the military, we're real losers. He's the winner, bathed in gold and strutting down Fifth Avenue. Tallulah's father is the hero; chopping up food for people, supporting his family even during this crisis. He kept going to work.

I wake up, make coffee and give the boys their cereal, and when Tallulah comes out for coffee, she says, "Mind if I check the news?" and I say, "Sure, not too loud, Sheryl usually is working." I feel like our conversation about race is so dark and heavy that it can't get heavier than whatever's on the news today, and we turn on the news to a white policeman killing a Black man in Minneapolis. Tallulah lets out a scream and Sheryl runs into the room. And then we all realize there are children, and we turn off the television.

"Just a moment," Sheryl says. I hear her tell the boys. "Do not come out of your room until I call you."

And we turn it on again, and we watch the whole thing. "I can't breathe," the dying man says. Tallulah stands up.

"I can't breathe," she says. "I can't breathe," she says
again. "He's telling that cop he's dying and that man doesn't
even care. He's just killing him." We're staring at the screen,
and it's insane that every adult in America is watching this
cop kill another man. So many police officers have gotten
away with so much brutality against people of color for
decades. So much redlining. So much injustice in the court-
room, in the classroom, in the job market, but this is right
on the street in broad daylight. There are people watching.
Someone is filming and this cop doesn't hesitate to kill
someone. It's like he's a robot and someone pushed the kill
switch. It's like what we've come to in America is these
people in the blue uniforms have gone to military training
and now they think they can kill people who might or might
not have known they were using a counterfeit twenty dollar
bill. The guy had survived Covid, but he didn't survive the
Minneapolis police department, the same police department that killed Philando Castile.

Tallulah lies down and begins sobbing, and I realize that
she probably has been taking care of her mother and hasn't
been able to cry for her father, and while she continues
crying, the newscaster in the background proceeds to tell us
that the man's name is George Floyd, that he was only forty-
six, that he had five children and two grandchildren. One
daughter was six years old. I take Tallulah in my arms and
then we are both crying. It's been so long since I hugged
anyone, and today we are not alone.

She says, "If there's a God, he wouldn't let this happen, I
can't keep going to church, and listening to the preacher

and sucking down this God business. Why does God let all this happen to Black people. God doesn't care."

And I say, "Are you still going to church?"

And she says, "I go to church online, but I'm done. I'm done with God."

"Myself, I never had any use for God," I say. "God doesn't see me. But I think God sees you. And I think you don't want to leave God behind."

"No, I'm done with God. God left me behind when he let that cop stand on that man's neck."

Her crying fills the room as if her father and God had left her in the moment, as if they had exited the scene taking her childhood with them.

"Tallulah," I say. "You gotta be you. I don't believe in God, but your grandmother is god-fearing. Your mama is god-fearing, and you pray before you eat. God didn't let that man step on George Floyd's neck. That man defied God and all that is good."

It's so odd that all of this is going down in Sheryl's house of all places. She brings over some Kleenex. It's strange how people will rise to a moment. She brings a glass of water. "Every time some white man puts their hand on a person of color to snatch their life, they are reaching into God to take away what God made. You are a prayer, you are a song, you are the beginning of the revolution; you are the change that is happening. Tallulah, my friend, God loves you." I don't have the right words, I feel like everything is coming out of me like salad.

"Thank you," Tallulah says, "I have to remember, I'm going to make things happen. And you? God loves you too."

I smile. "Maybe she does. She gave me a home."

"Really?"

"I'll tell you about it some other time, but I have a little yurt I live in now, it sounds weird, but it's very nice to have your own home." Tallulah says she's going to protest here in Los Angeles, and I say that I'll be there. Sheryl goes to the kitchen and makes hot chocolate, and we drink it and raise our cups to revolution, to George Floyd's family. Tallulah wants us to say a prayer for his family, and we all have a moment of silence to pray for them.

When she takes off, I make breakfast for the boys. I make them sausage, eggs, and pancakes. I talk to them and tell them to treat everyone with respect. I want to make sure they are kind to everyone. Kindness is underrated. In Corinthians, Paul says there are three great gifts, faith, hope and love and the greatest is love. I say forget them all. Give me kindness. Why can't we all be kind?

I don't know if I said anything right on this matter, in this moment. I can see Tallulah's face streaming with tears. I am only happy that she was with me and now, we will protest together. I am suddenly afraid of saying or doing or thinking the wrong thing in this brave new world and just as suddenly ashamed of thinking about myself at all.

CHAPTER 19

___

MAY 27TH

WHEN TALLULAH CALLS ME TO GO a protest in Downtown LA, I'm ready. I don't hesitate. I want to be part of something bigger. We plan to wear masks, but we're so angry, we have to go. She is going to make change happen. I can't change the world, but I don't want to sit on the sidelines. I don't want to be the girl who sat on the curb while the Berlin Wall fell down. I want to make history, so I tell her yes, I'm coming with you and we go. We march downtown, even briefly taking over the 101 freeway with hundreds of masked marchers. We march to City Hall. She hands me a sign that says, "Black Lives Matter." It's my first protest, so I forgot to make a sign. Sophia has made it clear that I need to leave by late afternoon. "The looting starts in the evening," she says.

"What looting?" I ask.

"The looting that's happening in Minneapolis is going to happen here," she says. "So get off the streets before sundown." I get home to my yurt and call Ed to see if needs me in the morning.

"What have you been up to today?" he asks.

"Here and there," I say.

"Protesting?"

"Maybe."

"Your first stop in the morning is Cedars. I'm calling now and we'll make sure you don't have Covid."

"Why's that?"

"You didn't think this through," he says. "I don't want to ruin your grand plan, but if you are going to be around children and old people, you need to know that you don't have Covid. So off to Cedars, I'll pay for them to give you a test and if you're negative, you can come by and you can go to your other jobs." He hangs up.

Nobody is ever proud of me, I think. Today, when I stood there with the protesters, I thought, we are pushing back against darkness, against the man stomping on people of color, and I'm here, and I'm doing it too, but now I'm not sure. I can't even protest for a day without risking my tiny livelihood. I call Tallulah.

"How are you doing?"

"I'm good, I'm here with my mom. You should come by and see her. Maybe Sunday."

"Okay," I say. "I'll come. You be safe. Thanks for inviting me today."

On Sunday night, when I'm visiting Tallulah and her mother, we watch the city burn on television. They live in Reseda in a small house with a backyard with tomatoes and chickens, and her mother, Shanice has a great laugh.

"There goes Forever 21," she says watching guys with boxes walking out of the store. "These guys aren't doing this in the name of George Floyd," she says, "those guys are just taking stuff. There goes the DMV. Up in flames. I hate the DMV. We all hate the DMV but come on. Okay, there goes Express. Such a bougie place. I can't find any clothes I like in there. Hot Topic? Remember when you used to like Hot Topic?"

"I did not like Hot Topic," Tallulah laughs. "That was a long time ago."

"Goth phase?" I ask. "*Lord of the Rings* phase?"

"I was into the baggy pants with chains," she says.

"Did you see the police car on fire earlier? In Beverly Hills?" I ask.

"Yeah, I'm sure the Beverly Hills people are worried," Shanice says. "This happened in '92. Only then most of the violence was in Black neighborhoods. Covid changes the game. People have been locked up a long time. People always like to ask why burn down your own neighborhood. Martin Luther King said it best: Riot is the language of the unheard. We've been lynched for too long and nobody's listening. And this," she waves at the television. "Yeah, a lot of this is just folks out there taking what they want. But what's behind this is a whole lot of anger over something real. Police brutality against Black and brown folks is real."

I feel like I could sit and listen to this woman forever. I get up and clean up from dinner while she keeps flipping from one news channel to the next. "Hey, Mia," she says. "While you're up, can you get some ice cream?"

"Mama," Tallulah says, "she's our guest."

"Hey, I'm honored," I say. I serve up vanilla ice cream and we all go back to the table.

When we eat, Mama Shanice says a prayer over the ice cream, and I feel blessed.

When I get ready to leave, she says, "Hang tight for a moment, I got something for you" and she gives me a dozen fresh eggs. She surprises me and gives me a hug before I leave. "You're a child of God," she says. "Don't forget it, he's watching over you."

"Mama, Mia here thinks God's a woman."

"Is God a white woman?"

"Hell, no," I say and catch myself. "My apologies." She laughs.

"I would hope not. Some stuck-up white bitch in the sky looking down her nose at us."

"I picture God a woman of color, she's Black, but she speaks a little Spanish too. She understands poor people and women of color and children and she hears us the most clearly. That's the God I pray too. The God the stockbrokers pray to is not my God."

"I hear you," she says. "Keep praying."

"Tallulah you keep in touch with this one and no looting you two."

"We aren't looting," Tallulah says. "We protest, we come home. Mia gotta work."

At home in my yurt, I put my eggs in my tiny fridge. I've bought one thing for myself that I'm pretty excited about. It's a tiny coffee maker. Now I can make myself coffee in the morning. I still buy Sophia coffee any morning we are cleaning houses together, but I can have a cup of coffee alone and watch the deer. I feel like I've given myself a cupful of happiness.

CHAPTER 20

JUNE 5TH

Tallulah wants to go to the Venice Beach protest which starts at 9 a.m. It seems like a good one to me because maybe we can socially distance on the beach. This turns out not to be the case, but I'm still glad I go. We march from Venice to the Santa Monica Pier. I don't have enough history with protests to have any clear notion of what we are accomplishing with this. But I realize that with ten days of protesting and the curfews going on at 6 p.m., that somebody must realize that something is wrong.

When I was at the cult, if you didn't get enough work done, the men would come in and beat us at the end of the day. And sometimes we would scream as loudly as we could, so they knew the beating was wrong. At least that's the point we wanted to make. Because silence didn't make the point. They just beat you until you lost consciousness. We tried screaming, and you'd think that having an eight-year-old or a ten-year-old screaming at the top of their lungs would be unbearable, but they would stop and wait until we screamed ourselves out and then continue beating until we lost consciousness. America, I think, are you waiting? Are you waiting until the screaming stops?

The next day, I go to Cedars for a test and then I call Ed. He gives me his grocery list and I go to Gelson's. When I arrive, he is sipping tea and eating sliced strawberries with crème fraîche. "Protesting again?" he asks.

"Yes," I say.

"You know I have three children," he says.

"You've mentioned that," I say. I want to follow up with a question, but we aren't friends like that.

"They don't come around because I was a terrible father."

"Terrible how?"

"I was awful. I can't even describe it. But you know, I've tried calling and I've told them I love them, and they don't want to talk. I don't get it. I'm their father. A little gratitude would be nice. I raised them."

"Did you? I'm just asking. Or did their mother?"

"Don't sass me."

I keep putting the groceries away neatly and I put away his dishes and plates.

"I'll be quiet, you do the talking," I say, and I think, *That's how men like it.*

"You get to ask questions. You've been very good to me. Juanita is out today by the way."

"So who raised them?"

"You're right, the nanny raised them. My wife was out sleeping with whoever. I was making money."

"That sounds standard rather than terrible. I mean your wife doesn't sound peachy. Where's the terrible part?"

"I withheld any love and affection. I was gone all the time and when I was around, I was cruel. But I want to make it up to them now. Why won't they let me?"

"I don't know them, so I haven't heard their side, I'm only hearing yours. But here's the deal; parents think that having their kids love them is a right. It's not a right. It's a glory. It's a gift." I pour him some tea. "You've been good to me, sir. And I appreciate it. I thank you for all of it. You've aged out of bad behavior maybe. But your kids don't see that. Think about it like this. When you're a sapling, you desperately need sunlight, air, water. You stripped away all that and your kids grew up spindly wanting all that love that makes us grow up healthy, and after you were out of the way, they went on with their lives and became themselves, thick trees in the woods and they didn't need you anymore. What do they do now?"

"My son is gay, and my two daughters, one's a doctor, one's in HR for a big film company."

"What does your son do besides being gay? Being gay isn't a vocation; it's his life."

"He's a lawyer. He didn't come out until he was in his twenties, I think he was afraid of me."

"What did you say to him?"

Suddenly Ed begins crying and I don't know what to do. I'm confused by emotions in men. The opera music is playing in the house, thick and heavy in the room, and I can hear his sobs. I'm lost now and I put my arms around him, and I know, whatever he did to this gay son wasn't good. He pulls himself together. "I've never told anyone, but I taunted him.

Of course I knew, and I thought if I said enough things to him, I'd snap him out of it."

"Snap him out of being gay?"

"Yeah. That was the plan. Night after night. Whenever I was home. I made fun of his speech. His clothes. His hair. I got the girls to join in."

"What is his name?"

"Frank, we called him Frank the Fag. We got him to dress up."

"*You* got him to dress him up."

"I'm sure he dreaded my coming home. My wife died when he was in college, but after he left for college, I never saw him again. When the girls left for college, I was invited to their weddings. I paid for their weddings, but then it was over. I think Frank and the girls are close, although I'm not sure. I'm shut out. I haven't seen any of them in years. But I want to make it up to them. I want to be a grandfather. I want to say I'm sorry for all those years. For everything. Why can't I be allowed to apologize?"

"You've tried to call?"

"No, I waited for them to call. I'm the father."

"Ed, I'm not a therapist. I'm not even a grown-up, so I'm going out on a limb here, but if my father is ever going to see me again in his entire life or my mother either, they would have to contact me and apologize. I'm done. I'm going on with my wonderful life. Who you are until your kids are twenty determines how they will treat you in the forty years that follow, that's a fact. Mine were horrible parents. I don't need them. You have enough money that your kids don't need to take care of you. If you were poor, you would have already called your kids and asked for a place to stay or a ride to the doctor, so the only reason you haven't called them is you haven't needed them. You're just waiting."

"What if they reject me?"

"Write a letter and beg each one of them for forgiveness. Trust me when I say this. If you were a shitty parent, your kids aren't going to come looking for you."

"I'm calling Frank," he says.

"Okay," I'll go outside and water the plants.

I WATER THE PLANTS AND WHEN I get back to the room where Ed is, he's off the phone and has gone into his bedroom. I finish up and get everything ready for afternoon tea and the doorbell rings. An incredibly handsome man is at the door. "Frank," I say.

"You must be Mia."

"He's resting," I say. "I can get you something. I'm getting the tea ready. I'll leave you alone when he comes down. How long can you stay?"

"I'll stay as long as I need to."

"Great, then I'll take off."

"He says this was your idea."

"I'm full of crazy ideas," I say. "I really hope this is okay. He's been good to me."

"We had some fun times. We used to play Charades, and he used to take us to Vegas once a year. I don't know why he thought that was an appropriate kid trip."

"He made it sound like it was cruelty by the minute."

Frank shakes his head. "He didn't win Dad of the Year, and I didn't think I would ever see him again, but my husband says to always give people a chance to change their mind about you."

"You look like him," I say. "I can see it; he still has the strong shoulders."

"When he was younger, yes. Mia, you take care of yourself," he says, and I turn to leave. "Here's my phone number, just in case you ever need to be in touch." He hands me a card. He's a lawyer with some big downtown law firm.

Ed comes down the stairs and at the sight of Frank, he begins sobbing as though his heart will break.

CHAPTER 21

JUNE 10TH

MY LIFE FEELS LIKE A WHIRL, like I'm dizzy. At some people's houses, there's a steady stream of news, coronavirus news. That's all they do is watch the death spiral of America; they keep track of how many people are dying; they watched the burials in New York in Potter's field in unmarked caskets, and they watch the stats rise nationwide. But always the endless obsession with the forty-fifth president, mostly with how he's trashing the nation. In California, most of the televisions are set on CNN and MSNBC and the news fixates on everything the president does wrong. I hate him, but I also hate thinking about him, I hate how he's always on our minds.

At other households, they seem more interested letting the kids watch YouTube videos and *Call of Duty Black Ops*, and it's like one long vacation from school. When Covid is over, a lot of American parents are going to find their kids missed that grade, but what can they do? Now they are having to be teachers and parents and they weren't prepared to be either, and even for the parents who are good parents, they can't zoom and care for their kids at the same time. Then there are the people hung on watching the protests and the looting.

"What is it with these people looting?" Chuck says.

"Why are white people looting?" I say. "Don't they have enough stuff? Look at that white woman looting Nordstrom, right there."

"There's plenty of Black looters," he says.

"What I don't understand," I say, "is when white people came here and took this country from the Native Americans and killed them, that was looting, that was stealing, that was white supremacy, and of course, four hundred years of slavery and oppression that's come after that, but you're really concerned about this looting?"

"You're too young to see the whole picture."

"Enlighten me."

"Don't get going on her," Sally says. "You leave her alone with your bullshit. Looting is wrong. Slavery was wrong, oppression is wrong. Wrongs don't add up to rights."

I'm folding clothes, and I need to move quickly because I still have the Royal house to clean after this. "You know, if you're a rich white person maybe you can't see what oppression looks like because you're wearing the oppressor's boots. It's like the cowboys used to say, 'the only good Indian is a dead Indian.' They wanted to exterminate everyone on the whole continent of North America."

"You know you're learning the wrong history," Chuck says. "America is a great nation. The greatest nation on earth. Everyone wants to come to America. Go someplace else. You'll see. You'll want to come home. It's because of this thing we have: freedom.

We've got freedom for everyone who lives in this great land. That's what makes America great." He stretches out on his couch, and his wife goes to the cabinet and gets him a pipe and some weed. "America is home to some of the smartest people on the planet." I'm finishing up, and I'm not sure if I want to respond. "Go ahead," he says. "I can tell you're thinking something."

"Oh, I'm thinking all right," I say. "But I'm thinking I should try to keep this job."

"I'm not going to fire you from cleaning my house for disagreeing with me. I don't care who cleans my house as long as they don't steal from me." Sophia takes off and I give her some avocados I bought for her.

"We aren't exceptional. We're the world bullies."

"Why don't you go live someplace else, how about Mexico? The average income is thirty-three hundred dollars a year. Why don't you move there? Or Guatemala? Or El Salvador? Get out if you want to criticize America. Love it or leave it. In this household, just so we're clear, we love America, and we love the current president."

"I know you love the president," I say. "No matter what he does, all his lying during Covid. You don't care."

"He's a great man," Chuck says. "If I thought it would make a difference, I would tell you that you had to vote for him, but California is a lost cause."

Sally walks me to my car, "I'm going to call you when he's golfing, so you don't have to see him anymore," she says.

"Appreciate that," I say.

"He gets worked up. It's his nature."

AT THE ROYAL HOUSE, I SET to work. Mr. Royal isn't there, and I get through the dishes, laundry, changing the beds and cleaning up, listening to my headphones, and going quickly from one room to another. When I get ready to leave, Mrs. Royal, asks me if I'll sit down to chat for a bit. "Can I clean up a minute?" I say. I go to the bathroom and wash my face. I'm thinner than ever, and I need a haircut, but so does everybody else. I could get Olivia to trim it this Saturday. She cuts everyone's hair in the family. I just don't want to ask too much of her. My hair is a curly mop down my back, but I usually keep it up with a stick and comb it out with a pick. The yurt has a small outdoor shower where the water is cold.

"What can I do for you?" I say.

"Could you look over this document and see if you think that you could have your godson's family sign it," she says. I glance over it quickly. It seems to indicate that they would be signing to say that they will never come after the Royal family for any paternity costs relating to the baby and I think this is a non-disclosure agreement as well, but I'm not sure. I've never seen an NDA, but I did learn about them in one of my classes, and I think this might be one. I put on my brightest smile.

"Sure," I say. "I'll take this to them. I see them Saturday."

"Okay, hopefully we can have this all signed by next week," she says. "Mr. Royal would like this resolved. And he says to tell you we can give you another five-hundred dollars for resolving this."

"Thank you," I say.

"You could keep it for yourself or for the baby," she says. "You know best."

"Okay," I say, and swivel out of there.

As soon as I get in the car and I'm driving, I dial Frank's number and he answers.

"Frank, this is Mia."

"Hello, I didn't expect to hear from you so soon. I had a wonderful visit with my father, and I think it's the beginning of something really beautiful, so thank you. I hope to see you again soon. Were you calling about something else?"

"Well, yes, I need help and I wondered if you could recommend someone to help me. It's a little complicated."

"When are you next at my dad's house?"

"Tomorrow morning."

"I'll be there. You can explain it then, does that work?"

"Yes," I say.

The next day, I'm delivering groceries when Frank arrives in his convertible BMW. I make tea and he and Ed sit down. It's funny how they have some of the same gestures. "Okay, so this is a little complicated. Your dad told you that I have this friend Sophia?"

"Yeah, he told me about your friends that you hang with."

"Well, my friends Olivia and Sophia were cleaning house for the Royal family."

"Richard Royal?"

"Yeah, you know him?"

"Yes, so continue."

"And his son convinced Olivia to go to Santa Barbara for the night and have sex, and she got pregnant and had a child

Juan, who is my godson. They're my family. I still clean the Royal house and they've seen the baby because I had to bring him along at one point."

"Oh my goodness. Richard Royal with a Salvadoran grandson," Frank says. "Do go on."

"Now they want Olivia and her parents to sign this," I hand over the document. He reads it.

"This is ridiculous. They are not signing this."

"He's my godson. I am trying to help them, and I don't know what to say to them."

"Where do they live?"

"The whole family lives in a one-bedroom apartment in Van Nuys, and it's really hard. It's twelve hundred a month rent, and Sophia's brother died. They are the only family I have. I just want to pay for a cheap legal person to help me. I was googling cheap legal help, but then I thought maybe you would have an idea. Because you know legal stuff; I saw your card."

Frank looks at his father. "Dick Royal, I'd love to shove it to him. I think I'll counter this and say that we are going to let the media know about this grandson unless he buys a house and sets up a college fund that we will administer, and he has to renounce any legal right to the child and then we will have our client sign the NDA. What do you think?"

"Excellent work, my son," Ed says smiling. "I love it."

"You, Frank?" I say. "You are going to do this? Richard Royal is friends with my father."

"Who is your father?" Frank asks.

"Thomas Alexander," I say.

"What a jerk. Well, I don't know that I can make him do anything, but I'll think about it."

"Do I have to go with you?" I ask.

"Not at all, I'll come by on Saturday to see your friends."

ON SATURDAY, FRANK ARRIVES IN A mask, and we all go to a nearby park so we can talk. He explains what he wants to do, and Sophia says. "What if they throw us out of the country? They said they would have us deported?"

"He can't do that. You are here legally. I'll make sure that doesn't happen."

"Okay," she says finally. "I trust you if Mia trusts you."

I DECIDE TO WAIT TO GO back to the Royals until they call me. She calls Monday. "So you hired a lawyer," she says.

"You didn't leave me much choice. You were going to give us five hundred dollars to raise a child."

"Don't ever come to our house again. Your days of cleaning our home are over. You are no longer welcome here."

"Ma'am, nobody ever starts crying when they can't clean your toilets anymore. Trust me, only in movies do people get excited when they get to clean up after other people. I will survive."

THE NEXT DAY WHEN I GO by Ed's, Frank is there. I tell them about the call. "I think she expected me to beg for my job or cry."

"How much money were you making?" Frank says.

"I was making six hundred a month," I say. "But I'm starting to get more tutoring and that pays better."

"Do you want to tutor our kids?" Frank says. "My husband needs a break once in a while."

"What if you bring those grandkids over here," Ed says. "I'm ready to meet them."

"They're loud," Frank says, "and they talk all the time because we don't have television, so they always want someone to tell them stories."

"Why are they not over here right now?" Ed says, and I think this is going to be very cool. "She can tutor them here at my house and give your husband a break."

"He might really love that," Frank says.

CHAPTER 22

JUNE 15TH

MRS. LIONEL NEEDS HER HAIRCUT, SHE says, and her nails done. I drive her to the nail salon, and we park around back. I call and let them know that we've arrived, and they let us in the back entrance. When we get inside, it's like a party in there. They've got black paper over the windows so no one can see in. "Why have I not been coming all along?" she says.

"Why not?" they say. "Lots of nail salons are open. We can't afford to be closed all year. This is ridiculous. If people can go to the grocery store, they should be able to get their nails done. We'll be bankrupt." Everyone she knows is at the salon getting manicures and pedicures, massages, and facials. They check your temperature when you come in, but they let me sit around and chat with her with my mask on of course, and pretty soon everyone is paying me to run to Starbucks and get the cold drinks. I earn one hundred dollars in the time it takes her to get a mani pedi. Then we're off to the hair salon. The reason she has me along to drive is that she's been taking a lot of Xanax because she says that she's lost money in the stock market and she's having anxiety attacks.

She has a cook at the house who makes the girls whatever they want at each meal. My job is to tutor them. Someone else takes care of the garden, someone takes care of the pool, and someone cleans the cars. One thing I'm always confused by is that when rich people say they are losing money, they never let anyone go. When I am feeling tight on money, and let's face it, that's all the time, I don't spend money on anything. She still has all these people showing up all the time.

We're on our way to her hair salon in Beverly Hills. She's lying back in the car resting. "Maybe I'll be okay," she says.

"I hope so," I say.

"Why don't you just say, 'I'm sure you will' like everyone else does."

"Well, I don't know enough about the economy or the stock market to be sure that you'll be okay, and I don't want to lie to you."

"My dear, life is a matter of lying. Life is all about lying. Tell me this. Am I beautiful?"

"Yes," I say. I tend to think everyone has their own beauty, and Mrs. Lionel with her dark red lips and thick hair certainly is beautiful.

"You could be beautiful as well," she says. "You need to learn about personal grooming. You need some lady-scaping."

"Whatever I need to do," I say. "I can't afford it."

"I wish I could just see you with a haircut," she says.

"I've always had friends snip it off. I've never been to a hairdresser."

"Oh, I guessed that. Where do you get your clothes?"

"I got both T-shirts and my jeans and my shorts at the Salvation Army."

"You have two outfits?"

"That's all I need."

"What do you wear to bed?"

"I have a T-shirt for that."

"What if you have a boyfriend over."

I smile. "I like your concern. That's when I bring out the sexy lingerie. No I'm just kidding. I never have a boyfriend over."

"Okay, seriously, I am having a little dinner party and I was hoping you could be there and meet my guests and watch the girls."

"Hello—Covid, are you not worried?"

"I'm so over the coronavirus. I mean, I was taking it seriously in March and April, but it's June now. It's just too much. People are out protesting. I should be able to have a dinner party and my friends are fine. We'll be outside. I need you to wear something though."

"Oh why, I want to be naked."

"You're a funny kid. I'll give you something. We'll check when I get home."

At the hair salon, we enter through a secret entrance in the alley, but once we get in, the lights are dim and the windows are all masked but it's super cool in there. They come right over and give us both a glass of champagne. Mrs. Lionel pops a Xanax and then says she will give them her card now in case she forgets later.

"Why don't you cut her hair too," she says. "Do you want a haircut?" I kind of do want to have my first haircut in this salon so that I won't look like a bush woman. "She tutors my kids, and I'm having a party, and I want her to look good. Do the whole thing," she says. They trim my hair, wax my eyebrows and I don't recognize myself. My hair is short and so cute on my head.

When we get back to the house, she takes out some cute pants and a top. "Try these on," she says. When I look in the mirror, I see that I look like an indoors person, like a normie. I'm surprised what a difference a haircut and clothing make.

I don't know how to thank her so I just say, "Thank you so much."

"You look very good," she says, but she seems a little zonked, so I leave her to pass out and go check on the girls.

AT THE DINNER PARTY, TWO COUPLES come over, and after I get the girls to bed, she tells me to come out back to hang out with them. I'm not used to hanging out with grown-ups, but I like observing married people. It's so strange to me that two people will choose to live together until they die. That's so long. If I were going to live with someone, it would be a girl. Men talk so much, and they expect women to do so much for them. I don't want to go from working for other people to waiting on people at home. These two couples, one a mixed-race couple, and the other a white couple seem pretty happy. Chloe is African American, and I note that she is the nicest to me. She goes out of her way to talk with me and ask my name. She and her husband seem to have a relationship of equals. He laughs at her jokes, and he claims to make less money than she does, but she says that he fixes everything around their house. "Once a plumber, always a plumber," he says.

The other couple seem a little squinty-eyed at each other. The man is wearing pretentious glasses. I keep thinking one too many glasses of wine, and one of them will say something they regret. Because I've been at so many people's houses, I've heard what they say behind locked doors, and I know that sometimes in public, they're all smiles, but in private, when just the maid is around, they get ugly. I've seen marriages where men are bullies and sometimes women are crazy.

"What's it like being home all the time?" Mrs. Lionel asks.

"I'm getting fat," the man with glasses says. "Susy keeps cooking me these nice dinners every night."

"When he was on the road," Susy says. "He was eating restaurant food. I'm cooking healthy food for him."

"Do you miss him traveling? Do you miss having your own space?"

"What she misses is my coming back with Louis Vuitton bags and diamonds;" he says. Susy takes a large sip of the red wine. I haven't had any. I need to stay sober. "She likes her jewelry." He says with a large laugh.

"No, no," she says. "You got me all wrong. I'm happy to be without the Louis Vuitton bags and jewelry. I'm relieved. You don't see me wearing any jewelry. You never see me using those bags."

"I thought all the ladies like Louis Vuitton."

"Did your friends tell you that buying purses and jewelry would make up for cheating? Because when you come back from a business trip, and you buy Louis Vuitton bags and jewelry that is an automatic red flag that you are cheating. I immediately go to check myself for STDs." Everyone stops drinking and eating.

"Have we had a little too much to drink?" he says. "Is it time to go home."

"Truth hurts," she says and stands up to finish off her wine in one large swill. I see them out the door and come back. Chloe and her husband are getting up to leave.

"I'm so sorry about that," Mrs. Lionel says.

"It's not your fault," Chloe says. She looks at me.

"This is my first dinner party," I say. "I guess it's good she didn't throw her wine at him. I'm just curious, do you all think they'll stay married?"

"Hard to say," Mrs. Lionel says. "But they might. They have kids. They have a lot of money. They might go to marriage therapy. He might stop cheating."

"You think he is cheating."

"Absolutely. Why else would he buy Louis Vuitton bags and jewelry?"

"I guess I don't see the point in staying, but I don't understand marriage at all. You guys seem happy though."

Chloe's husband smiles. "That's because she keeps me in line. We are attuned to each other. Some people get married to someone who they think they love, but it out turns out it's just someone they want to have sex with, and they keep staying, hoping that fun wild thing will keep them going. Big love takes work like growing a tree."

"Maybe I'll have my own tree someday," I say.

"Will your partner be male or female?" Chloe asks.

"Definitely a girl," I say. "Girls are yummy."

"I have a lot of queer friends."

"Can I meet some?"

"Let's make that happen." Chloe says.

She gives me an elbow bump on the way out the door and blows a kiss, and I think that her generosity just kills me.

CHAPTER 23

————

JULY 4TH

WHEN THEY SAY, "IT'S LIKE THE Fourth of July!" what
they mean is that it's a party. Sheryl has decided to spend
the Fourth with her husband in his hotel. I think they need
some time to do the wild thing, so I've asked if I can take
the twins over to meet the girls and she says, "Why not?"
Luke and Matthew have hardly seen any kids except each
other from March 15th to July 4th. I pull up at Mrs. Lionel's
house and take them around to the back gate to meet the
girls. They are eleven, and the girls are twelve and thirteen,
so I'm wondering how this age gap will work. The girls are
lounging by the pool when the boys come around the corner.
They head right for Mrs. Lionel. "Thank you so much for
inviting us for the Fourth," Matthew says.

"We're happy to help with the barbecuing," Luke adds.
"We're really very good at it. That's such a beautiful hat."

"Look at them working it," I think. The girls' mother
keeps sipping her bottle; she is always running off to one of
the pain centers and getting Vicodin. She has a large brown

bottle that she takes sips from all day, and eventually she nods off and I lead her off to her bedroom. Mrs. Lionel says that she was in a car accident and that's what led to the pain, and she hasn't been able to get off the stuff. When I ask where the dad is, Mrs. Lionel just says, he's a dirty cheater.

I'm worried that these girls will make fun of the twins, but as soon as they are all in the pool, it's clear, I need not have worried. "We should bring these boys over all the time," Mrs. Lionel says, "and by the way, call me Grace."

"Grace," I say. "Are you planning fireworks?"

"We'll be able to see plenty, don't worry," she says, and she's right. Their house has a great view of the city and from there you can see a mass of color. They've been going off for weeks.

"I don't understand. The mayor says no fireworks so suddenly everyone in LA goes to Nevada and buys fireworks, I mean, that's all I hear night after night."

"Wait until you see tonight."

I work with the kitchen staff and lay out the placemats, silverware, and napkins. I am eating with the kids, but Grace says no. The four kids are eating together and once I get their mother to bed, I get the kids to clean up their stuff. I can tell these four kids are going to get along just fine. They already have plans to play board games after dinner. "What are you going to play?" I ask the boys.

"Pandemic," they say together.

"You have to be kidding. You do know this isn't funny. Your father is trying to save lives right now, and this is serious business."

"We know that. We're just playing a board game out of respect. Seriously if you think we are disrespecting the dead, we can play Catan."

"You can play Pandemic. Just so that you remember to pray for everyone who is ill before you go to sleep."

"Yes, Mia," they say.

GRACE COMES IN AS THEY GO to get changed. "You can't wear that outfit," she says.

"You gave this to me," I say.

"But it's the same thing you wore the other night when they came over. They'll think you haven't changed your clothes."

"I'll tell them it's the only thing I have and that I washed them," I say cheerfully.

"Let's find you something else."

"I look cute in this."

"Come on." She finds an adorable dress. "I never wear this. Keep it. Do not sell it. So you can have it for dinner parties." The dress is yellow. I do look pretty zany in it.

"Got it," I say.

Chloe and her husband arrive, Chloe in a cloud of perfume. They have two friends with them—a chiropractor and a therapist—who seem to be long-time friends of Chloe's from college. They know Grace too. We start with a salad that's crab, avocado, and mango, and then we have wild rice and rare ahi. There's wine, and I'm spending the night, so I try some and it's yummy. I don't know how to talk conversationally with adults, so I'm afraid I'll say something wrong.

The chiropractor, Leslie, is sitting beside me and she's planning to take a Lyft home. We are eating out on the patio and it's getting dark, and the fireworks begin all across Los Angeles, a huge sparkling array. The kids come out on their deck to watch, and I see the boys are excited and the girls screaming. The dog keeps howling. I'm watching this one huge explosion that seems to be close to the house and I turn to see that Leslie, a creamy redhead, is watching me. I think, "Why is she watching me?"

Grace summons everyone to the kitchen to get their desserts and I am standing by the pool for a moment, and I turn to see Leslie still there and then she kisses me. *Wow*, I think, *I was not expecting that*, but I kiss her back, and then we go inside and Grace dishes up thick vanilla ice cream with a slab of melting chocolate brownie and chocolate sauce on top and whipped cream. When I step outside with mine, Leslie sits beside me, and I take a bite.

"Food of the gods," she says. "Grace is a magician."

"My mouth has had better," I say, "just a minute ago."

"Aren't you clever."

"I'm not clever at all. I pretty much never come up with anything."

"Well, you're a hell of a kisser."

"Then it's uphill from here because that was my first try, but I've been practicing on my arms because I don't have a pillow."

"Well let's get you a pillow."

"I think a pillow would be great to practice the kissing and the hugging, etcetera, etcetera."

"You are just adorable. Hand over your phone number. What is it that you do?"

"I tutor kids and I'm going to college. I want to learn how to save the world, but I'm very confused about what I should do."

"Take it easy, you've got time. How old are you, twenty?"

"I know, but you know that Martin Luther King was twenty-six when he finished his PhD. He was thirty-four when he delivered his 'I Have a Dream' speech. He had four children by that time. Kids my age live at home and plan to stay there through their twenties. They practice saying, 'hey boomer,' but what have they done? I want to be so much more than my fellow Gen Zers."

"Your fellow Gen Zers are changing the world in their own way. I'm an Xer myself. But don't doubt your generation. You guys are not watching Fox News. You believe climate change is real. You believe in gay rights. You want to change gun laws and legalize pot across the nation. Gay marriage is legal nationwide, who would have thought? Don't doubt your generation. Don't doubt yourself."

"Are you thinking I need to meet someone my own age?"

"I'm thinking you don't know what you want, but you'll figure it out." Lyft turns out to be expensive July 4th, but Chloe agrees to drive her home. We walk to the car first. She kisses me again, and this time, we get frisky with our tongues, and I start to see the sky rotate. While I clean up, the sky continues to shake with fallen stars and what with the wine and the taste of Leslie on my lips, I'm bumping around, and I can't stop smiling.

"I've never seen you like this," Grace says. I start laughing. "Good for you," she says.

The following week, Sheryl okays the boys coming for another swim. When I arrive, there's a big package for me that has shown up at Grace's house. I open it up. The smell of lavender hits me right away. It's a pillow. "Why is she sending you a pillow?" Grace asks.

"So I can sleep better," I say.

"Ah nice," Grace says. "What a lovely gesture."

CHAPTER 24

JULY 10TH

SOPHIA HAS GOTTEN OTHER WORK SO now I clean Chuck and Sally's house alone. When I pull up, I see both their cars in the driveway. Chuck has an old man's car, a silver Cadillac. You just can't picture anyone under one hundred driving a Cadillac. I picture old guys driving cars like that around Florida. In California, old men drive sports cars. Sally drives a new VW Bug and with her big chunky heels and dark hair with chunks of blue, she looks like an adventure. She meets me at the door. "He's here, but he's going to behave himself," she says. "It's too hot to play golf today and I can't send him anywhere, it's Covid and it's his house." Sally has large breasts and she always wears tops that show off her cleavage.

"Hey, I'm fine," I say, "I'm just the help."

"You are not," she says. I put on my headphones and get to work. Most people make more of a mess when they're home all the time but not these two. When Sally is home all the time, she must be cleaning a bit in each room. I keep my music going and my head down. When I'm finished, she invites me to a late lunch with them on the patio. I haven't eaten anything so I'm not turning down free food.

"Do you think you'll stay in California when you finish college?" Chuck says.

"I don't know," I say. "I hadn't thought of going anywhere, but I guess that's the great thing about America, you can move anywhere. California is the only state I've ever seen. I'd like to see New York. Especially the city. But I'd have to have a big job to live there, and I don't know if big jobs are in my future."

"What kind of jobs are in your future?"

"No idea. I'm confused especially because of the protests."

"What do you like doing?"

"Of all my different jobs, I like dog walking the best."

"That sounds like a winner," he says. "Dog walking. What are you going to college for? And who is paying for this?"

"I pay for myself."

"That's probably for the best."

"Don't torture her," Sally says. Sally eats salads, but Chuck and I are eating sandwiches.

"She'll know if she's being tortured," he says. "You know when I came to California from Texas during the energy crisis to work as an executive for Unocal, California still had that feeling of promise. People moved here because of the American dream. The California dream was like the American dream, only better. You didn't just dream of a house and a wife and a car. You dreamed of a house by the beach and a movie star wife with big breasts and your dog was going to be Lassie and you were going to live by the

Pacific Ocean and the trees by your house would be palm trees. You were going to wake up in Oz. The sex, the money, the orange trees with fruit in December. Florida had some of that same appeal but with crazy and hurricanes. California had it all, and you could change your name from Norma Jean to Marilyn Monroe or Marion Robert Morrison could become John Wayne."

"Was his name Marion?"

"Indeed. Try to imagine him making it in Hollywood as Marion, ah Maid Marion."

"Are you saying the American dream is wrecked or the California dream? Because I heard you used to be able to get free community college, that seems like it would have been great. When Pat Brown was governor."

"California has too many taxes, and too many immigrants. Los Angeles is less than half white."

"That's what I like about it. I mean I would be fine if it were a third white or a quarter white. The great thing about Los Angeles and San Francisco is the feeling that you're in these Pacific Rim cities that are bubbling with culture—all these different people and music and great ideas—and you feel like you are in a thought center, and anything could happen. It's like you're in the cauldron of the world."

"You haven't been anywhere, I get that. I'm going to patient with you. I've been to Texas and Vietnam and Florida and Oklahoma and Washington DC, so I'm going to tell you if you were living somewhere like Dallas let's say, I think you would really dig it. First of all, you'd be safe. You'd live in a white neighborhood. You'd marry some guy and take your kids to school and make dinners for him and have some office job. You'd be part of the American system of creating wealth, but that system would also be protecting you. Like an umbrella. You know how when you go to Orange County how everything is clean?"

"I noticed that. I went down to Newport Beach to take someone's dog to their beach house."

"That's because Republicans live there. Democrats are dirty."

I pause for a minute. I haven't registered for any parties, but I know if I did, I'm a dirty Democrat. "Why is LA so dirty?" I ask.

"I just told you, filthy Democrats run the city and let the homeless people run wild."

"Okay Chuck," Sally says.

"Wait," I say. "Did you know that by 2040, the US is going to be only fifty percent white? It's going to be fantastic. The whole country will start to be like Los Angeles."

"I hope I'm not alive to see that," he says.

"What if you guys who are watching Fox News came over to our side," I say.

"What side is that? Go out and protest? Because we're old and we don't want to catch Covid?"

"No, you don't have to protest. I was just thinking you could care about people and homeless people instead of money. I guess I understood that Republicans care about money and fear and Democrats care about people and the planet."

Chuck gets up and pours himself a drink. "Girlie," he says. "You don't even know what you don't know. I'll tell you what. When California is completely overrun with Salvadorans and

Mexicans and you have broken both legs and don't have health care, don't come running to me for help."

WHEN I LEAVE THEIR HOUSE, I go to see the new little pink house that the Royals' money has purchased for Sophia and Roberto. It is a three-bedroom house, and it has a little pool! I can't believe it. It needs a little work, but that will give something for Roberto to do. Before they moved in, he painted the inside of the house with his friends, and Juan's room has stars on the ceiling. I've brought a housewarming gift for Juan, a book case which Sheryl gave me and she gave me a bunch of books for it as well and I bought a Winnie the Pooh for him. It's a large bear and Juan starts hugging him right away. We get the bookcase set up. Roberto has been busy. He's built a bed for Juan and a bed frame for Olivia and one for he and Sophia. In the apartment, they slept on the floor, but now that they have a real house; they need beds. Frank comes by briefly and brings a barbecue, a nice one too, way nicer than we would have bought and Roberto, keeps saying, "This is too much!" but I can tell he can't wait to fire the thing up.

They have so few things, so Sophia already has everything unpacked. Their dishes are put away and their clothes are in the closets. Roberto walks me around and tells me his plans. He wants to make a nice patio area so they can eat outside. He wants to put out chairs and a table. He's trying to decide whether to make them or not. Between his friends and himself, they have a lot of tools, and now that he has a garage, he could start doing wood working and building furniture.

Then he will redo the kitchen and the bathrooms. The tiling, he'll get a friend to help with because he says tiling is tricky. The kitchen has layers of linoleum. "It has single pane windows," he says. "I have to replace those. I'm making a list and I'll fix everything one thing at a time as soon as I can afford them. I think I can fix everything in a couple years. Juan will inherit this house and Sophia is going to plant peppers and fruit trees."

We sit down for dinner and after the prayer, Sophia says, "Do you think it's wrong that we've been blessed with this house when so many people are dead?"

"Let's accept our blessings," I say. "As Tallulah would say, God knows what she's doing. The world is going through hell, and we received this tiny, good thing."

"I don't even think we deserved it," Sophia says.

Olivia has not spoken much since the baby was born, she's been very quiet. Sophia tried to get her to therapy at the free clinic, but Olivia wouldn't talk to a stranger, and they all agreed not to force her. She takes care of Juan, and she goes to school, but she's not the chatty funny girl I remember. I bring her things that I think she would like, and she nods, but I'm never even sure if she likes them, figs from someone's yard, flowers; she used to like cheese, so I try to buy her cheeses that she might like. Sophia says she takes a bite and that's all. She's far thinner than she was before the pregnancy.

We toast the house and Olivia says, "I'd like to say something. Mia, you're a good friend. You helped us get into a real house. Thank you," and I say, "Stop, I want to say something. I'm not the savior here. Sophia has been taking care of me and you all have been giving me a family, and that's why I've been okay and that's why I was able to meet Ed and Frank and it all looped around to you now having this house, but I say it was you all creating family that did it."

"To familia," Sophia says.

"I want to tell you what happened and then maybe I can start thinking about my life differently." She stands up and I suddenly realize how hunched over her thin shoulders have been. "We drove up the coast in his fancy car. I was elated. I have to say, I don't remember ever being happier. I kept wanting to pinch myself thinking this prince, this handsome rich boy is in love with me. He was singing along with the music. The music was all fun. There was some song about a good girl who wants to get nasty. Although I remember thinking that I didn't want to get nasty, but it was just a song. When we pulled up to Bacara, the hotel, I suddenly felt afraid. It was a big place, and I think I felt that I could get lost. I had a sort of fear of him leaving me in the room, going down to the bar. You probably remember, I had no luggage. We had left from his house. They asked for my luggage, and he laughed and that felt like I was a hooker. I started to feel worse. But he took my arm, and we went up to the people at the hotel and he was checking in and I was looking around at the flowers and the lights and people were looking at me. I was wearing shorts and flip flops."

I could see my little Olivia, her long beautiful hair, standing next to this rich boy in a hotel in Santa Barbara. How did that look? Did they look like a couple? Did she look like the nanny for kids he didn't have with him at that moment? Or did she look like he was bringing a woman to his room?

"We get to the room, and we can see the ocean, and I'm walking around the room, I'm excited. They have towels and bathrobes and little shampoos and conditioners and little soaps. I've never been in a hotel. Have you Mia?"

"I never have."

"They even have a little coffee maker and a little hair dryer, and he orders vodka and champagne and a hamburger, and he asks what I want to eat, and I say, I want a quesadilla. And he laughs and says, 'Of course, you want a quesadilla,' and it isn't a nice laugh, and I wish I'd ordered something more American like a tuna fish sandwich. What do American girls order? I don't know. Obviously not a quesadilla. He makes a few phone calls. Our food comes and I have a bit of the champagne and it's so sparkly in my mouth, and the quesadilla is okay, it's soggy, it's not like yours, Mama." Sophia puts her arm around Olivia. "Maybe I was feeling bold after the champagne, because I said something like let's go for a walk. I want to see around. And he'd had some vodka, and he was just like 'No, I'm not going anywhere with you.'" Olivia stops and gets something to drink. "That's when it started to get bad. On the way up, he'd said, 'We should go to Paris sometime. We should go to London.' And I had started to think we were dating. I was his girlfriend. I was thinking I was going to introduce him to you, Papa." I can tell this is very painful for Roberto, but the man is solid. He knows his daughter needs to tell this story and he is sitting there. Sophia hands him a cup of coffee black.

"He said we weren't going anywhere. There were friends of his at the hotel and then I said I wanted to meet them, and he said, 'You little whore, you aren't meeting anybody.' The next thing I knew he was on top of me. It happened so quickly it's hard to even to explain. I was completely unprepared. I had thought, I'm sure he has condoms. He seems like a man of the world. Dad, I'm so sorry. Mom, I'm so sorry."

Sophia and Roberto immediately take her in their arms, and we are all crying. "You have nothing to apologize for," Roberto says. "Nothing. Believing a man is not a crime. Please m'hija, I love you. You made a mistake to get in the car with that monster. You do not owe me or your mother an apology."

"I have been thinking you guys thought I was such a terrible person."

"You listen here," Sophia says. "What kind of parents would we be if we blame our children when someone wrongs them? You are not at fault here. We love you. We want you to find happiness."

"What if I don't?"

"How do you feel now?"

"I'm happy because you all love me."

"You know," I say to her, "a lot of people are lonely all the time. Because they're separate from each other, and they can't forgive each other, this is what we have, familia, I'm so lucky that you invited me into yours, and I think a loving family is the best happiness. So maybe you already found happiness."

Sophia gets three candles and lights them. She looks at her daughter. "This one is for our family, this candle is for Juan being everything he can be, and this one you are going to blow out and let go of the story of shame and we'll be done with it. And any time it comes up, you come to me, we light a candle, we say a prayer for you, for our family, for Juan's great life and then we say goodbye to that story because bad stories sometimes want to hang around, you have to say goodbye to them a few times and then finally they're gone."

Olivia blows the candle, and the other two candles shine on their small table and her face is wet with tears. While I'm driving home, I keep thinking, how did I fall into such a cradle of love?

CHAPTER 25

JULY 15TH

THE ONLY WAYS PEOPLE CAN CONTACT me are email, phone, and snail mail because I have a post office box. I like to be able to get mail and to have a real mailing address. I figured out almost immediately when I started to get work, that you need a real address. It was bad enough not to have a street address. I'd like a real address. It makes me so happy that Sophia and Roberto have a house, I could have my mail sent there, but I don't want to presume. My P.O. box is working fine. At least as long as anyone in the country is getting mail. The president has been threatening to shut down the mail and saying Americans don't need it anymore. I can't believe that there are people in America that still like him, I just don't see it. He's a big liar. I'm picking up my mail one day and getting ready to go to Vallarta to get the ingredients for salsa and tamales to take to Sophia's. I'm in a pretty good mood. I'm saving well toward UCLA. My car had to go to the shop, but my guy was able to fix it for less than two hundred dollars, so when I see that there is a letter from Santa Cruz, I think, "No, no, no. How did you find me?"

I'm not that hard to find. In the old days, people used to hire private detectives to find missing people. Now, you just scramble around the internet and voila you know where someone's house is and how much it's worth. *"Dear Mia,"* my mother writes. *"You need to call me. Half of us have Covid, and the other half will soon. It's all this living together, cooking together, and sleeping together. Y is dead of Covid and three other people too. I haven't gotten it yet, but I need to leave. I need you to take care of me. I have always loved you. I love you so much. I can't even describe how much I love you. Call me and tell me where you are, and I will come to you. Your loving mother."*

All I can think is thank God I don't have a social media presence. There are no pictures of me on Facebook or Instagram or she would be at my door right now. Her love for me is as deep as her own need for help. When I was young and needed protection, she needed to have fun. She was screwing the guys in the cult and doing drugs and dreading her hair and dancing around the campfire. But now, her love is like a rope of need. If you take care of your children, and you do your best as a parent, then you've built them a boat and they will build you a boat. But if you're asking for a boat when you let them go under, that's not love, that's raw need, that's a potato in the ground seeking sunlight. But I don't have an answer, and if I ignore her, she'll get aggressive. The letters will cascade, and she will begin the search. She'll find me. She's probably in San Francisco now. I call Ed and explain the situation.

"Come on over," he says. "Frank's here."

Frank and Ed read the letter. "She'll find me eventually," I say. "It's just a matter of when. She's gotten to the Bay already, and she's going to ask around there and eventually someone will have seen me and will know I left the city, and she'll figure out I'm here, and then she'll come and she won't stop. If she gets here, she'll expect me to take of her."

"You don't have to do anything," Ed says.

"Yes, but she's going to show up at my yurt and then she'll demand whatever money I have, and of course I'm going to say no, but she'll be merciless, and she'll start following me and wanting to go to jobs with me."

"How do you know all this?"

"Because she's my mother, and she's crazy and she left once before when my uncle was there, and he left and then she came back."

"Wait, you have an uncle? Let's contact him."

"He won't have anything to do with her. He and I have never spoken. That's why I never mentioned him. He's not part of my life."

"Do you have his name or number?"

"Yeah, I took it from her before I left."

Frank dials the number while he looks the name up. I'm so sick to my stomach that I can't stand it. I go and throw up while he begins the conversation with my uncle. I met him once while I was still with Y and then he left. When I come back, Ed tells me to lie down on the couch and take it easy. But I can't take it easy. My mother wants to ruin my life. I can't think of anything worse than having her come and live with me. I'll die. I sit up. "I'm ready to be part of this conversation," I say.

Frank puts me on speaker phone. "Hello James," I say. "Long time no speak?"

"Your dad and I talk from time to time."

"Oh, are you friendly with him?" I ask. "James, I am living in Los Angeles and going to college."

"What can I do for you?"

"My mother wants to come live with me, and I can't take care of her. I need you to help out."

"Okay, I can do that. I am sorry I haven't been in touch. I never got to know you. I do have a friend with a mobile home park in Florida where I might be able to get her settled. Can you text me her phone number?"

JAMES AGREES TO CALL ME BACK, so I don't have to deal with her at all. I thank Frank and Ed, and I feel foolish because it seems like I could have solved this alone. Within a week, James has flown my mother to Jacksonville, Florida and from there, had someone drive her to Crystal Springs Estates where he has bought her a mobile home. I am so relieved. James meets me at Ed's house the next week.

"Hey niece," he says when I walk in. He's wearing a suit and drives an Audi.

"Hello," I say, "Well didn't you turn out fancy?"

"Fancy is as fancy does," he says. "Mother used to always say that."

"I remember, when you asked her for pretty much anything. Like can I have socks? Oh, you want socks. Well *la-di-da*, fancy is as fancy does."

He laughs. "Nice to finally really meet you," he says. He thanks Frank and Ed, and we all sit down outside. "So, I got to tell you," he says. "I call her, and she says, 'Brother, I miss you, I love you so much,' etcetera. She starts weeping. And I say, Sister, if you stop crying, I'll buy you a house. Then she stops flat right away. I say, I'll have a car come for you. We'll test you for Covid, if you don't have it, I'll put you on a plane to Florida where I've bought you a house and it's all ready for you. And she's like, okay. She packs her bags in a minute, and I get her tested and fly her from SFO to Florida, but it gets better. She brings a dog with her. I don't know even know where she found this mutt, but she arrives with some hound and the Crystal Estates only allows dogs thirty pounds or less. So, get this, I love dogs but I'm not bringing her back to California to live with me. I had flashes of what can I do to this dog to make it weigh thirty pounds? I have this house completely ready for her. Food in the fridge. She's four miles from the grocery store, but she can take a cab once a week. The place has a pool, she's set but she arrived at this place with a German Shepherd."

"Oh my God," I say. "What did you do?"

"I had the driver take her to a Days Inn by the airport that takes dogs. I left her there for two days without calling her and I didn't return her calls. I just had the hotel staff put pictures of Crystal Springs under her door. I paid one of the hotel staff one thousand dollars to adopt the dog and find her a smaller dog."

"You did not."

"Desperate times."

"Let me see her new dog."

"You bet I have a picture." He brings out his phone. The dog has beady eyes, foolish ears, a silly smile, a short tail, and a round body.

"What is it?"

"You have to hear it," he says and plays the video. "It's a Chihuahua pug." On the video we can hear yapping going on and on.

"Did she say whether she would miss us?"

"You know, I have a client in Jacksonville, he's already been by to check on her once. I had put some furniture in the mobile home and a big mirror in the living room. She was looking at herself in that mirror when he got there, and he asked if she needed anything, and she said, 'Not a thing.' She was playing with the dog and watching television and drinking wine in the afternoon."

"I hope the dog keeps barking," I say. "Has she ever had a job?"

James laughs, "Your mother was always planning to be whisked away. What's your plan?"

"She's fine," Ed says. "She's going places." As I drive home, I keep thinking of my mother who has somehow managed the world, so she's never had to work at all. I don't want to be her because if you never do anything you never get to be anything.

CHAPTER 26

JULY 20TH

I'M CLEANING A NEW PERSON'S HOUSE in Granada Hills which is at the top of the Valley. Her house is on Louise and it's quite large and has pillars like it's supposed to be an Italian villa or something. I showed Ed where this house was and we looked it up on Zillow and it's worth a couple million, but it's in a dumpy little part of the Valley. I guess you could be rich and incognito. While I am cleaning, the owner, Regina is telling me about this friend of hers in the neighborhood who owns a really big house, and she asks if I see want to see it, and I have to pretend that I do because I can tell she really wants to show me, so she buzzes me over there and this house, also in Granada Hills is ten thousand square feet. I mean if you lived in Bel Air, sure, but this is a neighborhood where people send their kids to public schools and leave mattresses on the curb. The huge house has a pool, and massive closets that are as large as where I live. The kitchen looks like nobody cooks there. Regina says they order their food from Grubhub. The house smells like artificial flowers. Regina is friends with Sheryl and I'm helping her while Regina's housekeeper is on vacation.

She has friends over while I clean, and they talk by the pool. Mostly they talk about stuff they see on the internet and when I am in the room, they like to ask my opinion as well. It's odd to me that nearly the whole time I'm at their house they are on their phones, and they are complaining about the stuff they are seeing on their phones. They bitch about Facebook and Twitter. They almost never take their eyes off the screen. I sometimes wonder what they would do if they lost cell phone coverage and they had to talk with each other without their cell phones. They like an app called Nextdoor, but it makes them angry as well.

"You know what someone posted today," Regina says, "They posted: We are having a celebration for our police station. What are you deplorables going to do for the Devonshire Police Station?"

"What does that mean?" her friend asks.

"I don't understand," Regina says. "If you are calling someone 'deplorable,' you aren't going to get them to throw a party for the police and seriously who is throwing a party for the police right now? People post on Nextdoor all this bullshit complaining about homeless people. It's mean. What do you think, Mia?"

What I'm wondering is if they know how close to homeless I am. "Why do you look at the Nextdoor?" I ask. "Maybe you should delete the app if it's annoying you."

Her friend laughs. "She makes a good point Regina, you do nothing but complain about it."

"People never have nice things to say. It's like Facebook. God, I hate Facebook. Which is almost as bad as Twitter. Twitter is just like you put a bunch of monsters in a room and gave them rocks to throw at each other. Starting with the president."

Regina sends me home with apricots from her tree. As soon as I get into my car, I start eating the apricots. There's nothing like fruit right off the tree. Regina is going to make jam as well, and she says she will give me some. I like to think of myself eating apricot jam and bread in my yurt and maybe I could get a toaster. A toaster would be such a wonderful thing. I keep thinking about waking up to toast. I don't want to be like the Karens always wanting more and more. I worry about developing needs.

AFTER WORK, I GO TO TALLULAH'S house. Her mother is making dinner for us and as soon as I walk in, I can smell the dirty rice and shrimp gumbo. Her mom is from the South, and she can cook up some Louisiana cooking that makes you cry with happiness. Tallulah and I sit outside on their little picnic table drinking beer. She's been tracking a lot of the police violence since George Floyd, and she shows me some of the videos. She has a plan that involves rallying students of color in Los Angeles to demand justice and to demand change in the Los Angeles Police force.

"I want permanent change to the police force. All this stuff was happening when Mama was a girl," she says.

"I have a question, or rather two. I was cleaning house for this lady today and she seems like she means well. She says that she posted Black Lives Matter on her Facebook and her

Instagram and she and her friend who were drinking wine spritzers while I cleaned the house were talking about how nasty it is to say bad things about the homeless or good things about the police on Nextdoor. What would you say to Regina and her friend Karen?"

"Ah the Karens of the world," Tallulah says. "It sounds like she means well. Posting BLM on her FB and her Insta feels good for her."

"She never watches Fox News. She teaches at Cal State Northridge, but seriously what does it do for her to post on Instagram?"

"She's an armchair intellectual. She cares from a safe distance. That's most people, honey. She votes, but that's where her engagement probably stops. Maybe she convinces her students to think differently. What does she teach?"

"English."

"Well, maybe she's teaching critical thinking."

"That's her story. I shouldn't even be worrying about her."

"No, it's natural to try to figure stuff out, and to figure out what you might want to do yourself. By the way, do you ever get time off?"

"Yeah, I'm taking this coming weekend off, just to breathe, why?"

"Well, I'm going out with a few women to Joshua Tree. I know it sounds Covid crazy, but we're going to stay in this friend of mine's place. I just want to get out of town. I'm inviting a few girls who have been pretty much podded down. My friend has a big yurt and smaller little yurts, and we are going to meditate. You want to come?"

"Sure, is it free?"

"Yep, none of us have any money. We just bring food."

"That I can manage."

"Sure, because you don't eat anything."

"I do too. I'm about to eat a bunch of your mom's food."

"Sometimes I think you don't eat except here and Sophia's house. In between, what do you eat? An apple a day?" She's laughing.

Her mother comes out and serves dinner and we sit down to eat. Her mom's shrimp gumbo can't possibly be good for you. I'm going to guess there's a lot of butter happening. She's also made this crusty yummy bread and coleslaw. The whole meal is delicious.

Once her mom is eating, I say, "I have something for you guys, and I wanted to wait for dinner to bring it out. I got a basket of avocados for you."

"Girl, you didn't have to do this," her mother says holding them up. "These are nice. I'm going to make some fine guacamole."

"So what happened that you stopped writing for the campus paper?" I ask.

"I had written an article about how the African American students at Pierce make up almost ten percent of the student population versus Valley College where the population is less than five percent and I said that Pierce is a better college to go if you're Black because there is more support for African American students. It was an opinion piece, and that was my opinion. The next thing you know people are writing hate pieces, threatening to kill me and we had to take the piece down and I stopped being a writer altogether."

"So, you quit the paper?"

"Yeah, I was done."

"I'm really sorry."

"I stopped writing. I don't trust anybody at this point except you, Mom, and a couple other people."

"I get it," I say. Her mom has made a peach pie for dessert from the peach tree in their yard. When I bite into that peach pie, I say to her mom, "Okay, I'm moving in." Her mom laughs.

WE GET TO JOSHUA TREE ON Friday. I drive out with Tallulah who sings all the way out to Prince and Janet Jackson, but when we arrive, it's quiet. I keep wondering if this is a great idea. If I get Covid, I am going to really regret it because I'm going to lose work. But I'm ready for life in a yurt. I have a sleeping bag, and I'm ready for an outdoor shower and a campfire. Some of the girls are a little thrown and keep calling the situation primitive. We meditate and then hike the first day and tell stories that night while cooking s'mores. Saturday night there's a lot of drinking and around midnight everyone is passed out except Tallulah and me. We take flashlights and go walking out among the Joshua Trees which look like huge people populating the landscape.

"What are you going to do?" she says.

"You know you were talking about writing," I say, "and all the abuse that got hurled at you. I was thinking if there's no money in writing, no future, no way up, no recognition, I think that's the thing for me. I like the idea of doing something where I'm not going to make money but I can have a voice. I want to be like a salamander; the California slender salamander has no lungs; they breathe through their skin. I am going to take in all the stories I can and write them down. I'm not going to breathe; I'm going to absorb."

"I brought a comforter," Tallulah says. "Come here." We lie down together on the comforter, and it's big enough that we fold it on top of us, and we have a pillow that we share. What we see is the Milky Way, so much bigger than I've ever seen it, a luminescent blanket of stars, a stain of white creamed across the sky. She takes my hand. "You write," she says, "the stories that get under your skin, and listen to the music. The music of the stories. Get the notes right. We aren't free. We aren't brave. The cowboys didn't come on horses to rescue us." We're quiet for a long time, and we see falling stars. "They're not falling stars," she says; "it's a meteorite shower. Scraps of dust falling to earth."

"Is home wherever your mom is?"

"Yeah, she's home, what about you?"

"Sophia's house is a place for me, but not a home; my car is my home. But I think I'm going to claim this place. I'm going to come back here when I'm lost. To this sky and remember opening my eyes into all this, the red giants, the planets, the white dwarfs, the white swarm of stars that make up the Milky Way."

"You know the petroglyphs we saw today left by the Native Americans, I loved those. I keep thinking how they were connected to everything here," Tallulah says quietly.

"Your mother would say connection with others is our natural state, but dominant cultures fight it because they don't want to have to give." I say.

"We can't change history," she says. "But we can make a new future. We can be new baby stars blazing across the galaxy. I'm waking people. You're writing everything down."

"Okay," I say, "This is our go to place. We have to come back here and remember where we were born."

CHAPTER 27

AUGUST 3RD

I SHOW UP TO CLEAN REGINA's house, and she tells me that Laura, the owner of the ten-thousand square foot house, wants me to clean their house too. I am always squeezing in clients, so mask and cleaning supplies in hand, I show up to clean the mansion the following week. I called and asked if I could bring Sophia, but Laura said she only wanted one person. It had seemed so immaculate that I hoped it wouldn't take long to clean. They said to arrive at nine in the morning, but I like to arrive early for jobs, so I get there at 8:30 a.m. When I ring the doorbell, nobody answers. People keep odd hours during Covid. More people stay up late and sleep in, I've noticed. I wait outside. Fifteen minutes later, Laura opens the door. "Sorry, that took so long," she says.

"We were sleeping in our bunker."

"Sure," I say, "of course."

"Do you want to see it?"

"Love to." We go through the house with its huge chande-liers, its massive paintings, its carpets, and its gleaming kitchen, and out into the backyard. There's a porthole she opens to a set of stairs. We go down the stairs to a door that closes with an airtight whoosh.

"In here we are safe from Covid and everything," she says, "so we like to sleep down here sometimes to just get used to it. It's a lot like her upstairs house, only smaller." The kitchen is laid out nicely. I go from room to room. There's a TV room, a bathroom, bedrooms, a laundry room. "Actually, if you can clean up a bit in here, that would be great," she says, "the rest of the house is not that dirty. I'll turn on some music here. What do you like?"

"Tom Waits?"

"Tom Waits Pandora," she says and the music leaps to life in the bunker. "Even if there were no internet, it would keep running from memory," she says. "We have backup generators of course. My husband started researching these and he realized that three million Americans have bunkers and let's face it, three million people can't be wrong. Bill Gates has several of these bunkers. Having just one frankly leaves us vulnerable every time we travel. I'm guessing Bill Gates is never far from one of his bunkers. You have to think about the future. This is a good lesson for you. Look around, cleaning this part shouldn't take long. We just sleep here."

Left alone, I check the place out. There's a room with a pool table; there's a greenhouse in one room; there's a room for doing wood working; there's a jacuzzi down here. This underground house is much better than most people's houses. I feel like I've begun to understand something about the one percent, they're afraid to die.

When I get finished and come in, I start with the kitchen and Laura's husband walks in naked. I apologize for being there. "Don't apologize," he says. "My wife is the one who insists on having a cleaning girl; I've told her that if we have to have someone, I'm going to walk around the house naked anyway."

I turn to him and look him straight on. "Of course, sir," I say. "It's your house, you should dress as you wish."

"There's the spirit," he says. "Make sure you mop away all the little bugs. My wife is terrified of spiders."

"I like the bunker," I say. "It's impressive."

"Did you see the pool in the bunker?"

"No, I did not."

"Well, it has one, I have everything in that bunker, it's ready to go. Mind you, I do not want to have to live there. I want to live here, but it's always good to be ready."

"Do you use it as a guest house?"

"We don't have friends stay with us," he says shortly. He takes his coffee and goes out to the backyard and stands by the fountain.

Laura wanders around in a bathrobe while I'm cleaning. "I want the house clean because the children are coming back today," she says. "Do you think I've taken too much Xanax?"

"How much did you take?"

"I took about three pills, maybe thirty milligrams?"

I google "normal dose of Xanax.," and I look at her eyes which look pretty glassy. "Yeah, I think you overdid it," I say. "Why are you sucking down Xanax?"

"I'm so anxious. Come on, here we are with Covid and the riots and so much shit going wrong in 2020, I can't take it and then my kids were taken away. They're bringing them back today, but I need to show that we're responsible parents."

I keep polishing the furniture. "How do your kids get taken away from a house like this during a pandemic?"

"My daughter called Child Protective Services because she said her brother was making her give him blowjobs and she made it sound like we knew about it, but we didn't. We didn't know, and we had to get a lawyer and now they're coming back and we're having them go to therapy. We didn't know." She keeps following me while I clean the bathrooms.

"When are they going to get here?"

"At 2 p.m.," she says.

"Okay," I say. "You should see if you can sleep off the Xanax. How long does it take you to wake up and get dressed and everything?"

"Hour and a half if I have coffee."

"Okay, where do you want to sleep?"

"The bunker."

"Okay, I come get you in the bunker at 12:30, you'll have time to sleep off some of this."

By 2 p.m., the house is clean. She gives me an outfit of her clothing and I do a quick shower and change. I open the door when the woman from CPS arrives with the two kids who are tall and very good looking. I introduce myself as the newly hired children's tutor and I show her into the living room. After an interview with the parents, she asks to speak to me. She asks for references, and I give her mine. She takes my phone number. "I'm going to need to check in with you," she says.

"Absolutely," I say.

"It's good to have an independent observer in the home," she says.

"Certainly," I say.

When she leaves, the children meet me, but they seem eager to go swim in the pool. They avoid talking with their parents. I'm packed and ready to go.

"Can we talk with you before you leave," the father asks.

"Sure," I say.

"What do you do for a living?"

"Mostly I tutor; I clean a few houses. I do some errands."

"Can you tutor our kids? Just make sure they are doing their homework? We'll pay you whatever you charge. But we want to know if anything weird is happening."

"Like what was happening before?"

"Yes."

"May I ask why she didn't come to you?"

"Kids these days," he says. "These two were my wife's idea, but I'm not going to jail for them. I mean, I like them and all, it's just this is too much. I've just spent thousands on attorneys. You make friends with her, so she'll talk to you next time. You got it."

"I'll do my best," I say.

When I leave there's a text for me to stop by Sophia's house; there's a package for me there. When I arrive, Leslie is sitting on their front step.

"What are you doing here?" I ask.

"I know where you hang," she says. "How's the pillow?"

"Have you ever thought that there are a lot of crazy people in the world?"

"Yeah, today a bad day?"

"Pretty much."

"Because I was thinking I could follow you home and we could have a picnic."

"Did you bring the picnic?"

"Yes, I did."

When we get to my place, we spread out her quilt and there's pasta salad and drumsticks, grapes and cheese, a baguette, and a beer for each of us, I can't stop smiling. I turn on Nina Simone Pandora. I light a candle. We get up and dance.

"Save some room," she says, "I got us some carrot cake, and you don't know what's happening to you next. There are consequences for walking around the world like you do and today's the day when you get to find out those consequences." There's a slight shudder in the trees, and Nina Simone keeps wailing. I can hear the wolf walk above us. The moon is full and heavy, a swarm of yellow light all over the bed like honey.

CHAPTER 28

AUGUST 7TH

I GET A CALL AT WORK on Friday from my friend Tony. Tony is a person I keep in a small secret part of myself. I never tell anyone about Tony, my connection to my brother, Adam. I am deeply ashamed of Adam who is sliding helplessly down the throat of Los Angeles into the hellscape at the bottom. While I struggle from car to yurt perhaps back to car again, Adam spirals, and I visit and watch the unravelling.

He lives down at Skid Row and he and I used to hang out together sometimes when I lived in my car. I would get stuff for him, and he would always let me know what was going on with my brother. When Adam got to the age where the boys were briskly raping the girls and cleaning their teeth after, he ran away. I never thought I would see him again, but when I was in Downtown LA buying flowers at the Flower Market for one of the ladies I work for, I saw this young man who I thought might be him. This was last year. I followed him to this trap house, dark, a couple trap girls sitting around glassy eyed told me to shoo. As I came out, I ran into Tony in a wheelchair.

"What are you doing girlie girl? You don't belong here. You gonna get yourself in trouble."

"My brother's in there," I said.

"You can't help him," he said.

"You live around here?"

"Come on." Tony took me to his tent which was set up private like away from the other rows of tents. I took him to lunch, and I heard his whole story. He was a vet; he didn't want to live indoors. He thought the government was watching him. He still got a check from the government and with that check, he bought food for himself, and his dog Charles and he bought weed and booze. I asked if I gave him a little money if he would keep an eye on my brother and he said he would. I did get to talk with my brother a couple times, and once we went to lunch, but he didn't eat, and he didn't seem able to concentrate. He asked if I had any money. Tony, true to his word, kept track. I know every addict has some moment that they hit rock bottom and surely, my brother would have that moment, and I would be there for him. Every month, Tony would send me a picture of my brother, once he was passed out with a needle in his arm, sometimes he was with another man. I remember my brother as beautiful with long lashes and a high clear singing voice, I remember the girls all loved him and thought he loved them. In the pictures sometimes he and a man are kissing. Sometimes they look happy. In each picture, I can see the heroin taking hold. As for Tony, I would send him twenty bucks.

Before Covid, we went to lunch once a month as well, but since Covid, I've been sending him a little extra for lunch.

I'm worried about the downtown homeless population and the coronavirus. Los Angeles has almost 60,000 homeless people and a lot of them are crowded in tents on the city sidewalks in downtown. When you come to LA to sight see, that's what you see, tent cities of people living on the street. In some future world, we will look back on the early 21st century, and we'll say, yeah, that was us, we were just stepping over people to get to Starbucks. Our government was making smart bombs while people lived in the streets.

Tony calls me and says you need to come now and then he hangs up. I go. He's given me an address. I'm thinking maybe my brother is ready to clean up, sober up. As I'm driving, I'm thinking about whether I can get him into a free rehab during Covid. When I arrive, Tony is in his wheelchair waiting for me. He doesn't say anything, so I just follow him down Beaudry and into a construction site. My brother is there, and I'm not sure how long he's been dead. He was beaten about the head and shoulders and laid over the rails of the site. He has no shirt, no belt, no shoes. I'm not ready for this. I collapse on the street, rocking back and forth. I'm moaning like I used to as a child during the long nights sleeping in a large room with the other girls on the floor with no parents, we moaned ourselves to sleep. Orphan rock. I can hear myself like a wild animal.

Tony says, "Honey, I can't be here when you call 911. I'm off grid. You gotta call, girlie. You gotta call. You got your whole life to cry. I'll be here for you, me and Charles. We're always here for you, but you gotta call. Stand up. Drink this and call." He hands me something. It doesn't occur to me until later, what mercy made him prepare a cup of coffee for me. I drink the coffee. I call. The police arrive. Then the coroner. I have his body taken to the same mortuary in the Valley as Sophia's brother was taken.

I call my mother. She does not answer. I leave a message. "Your son is dead." I call the father. I leave a message. "Your son is dead." I always wondered why he didn't come back for Adam.

My father took Adam for the day to San Francisco once when I was small. I begged to go along, and he just laughed. When he brought him back to Y, he told my mother, she says, that he could care less about having a boy like that. When I have Adam's ashes, I will take them to San Francisco and throw them into the Bay. If he could have lived and loved, it would have been in that city, celebrated, walking down Folsom Street on a spring morning with a lover singing "Guys and Dolls" like he used to sing for us.

OLIVIA AND TALLULAH ARE COMING TO my yurt to spend the night and we are going to have a ceremony. I have herbs and tomatoes in pots, and we are going to use some herbs in our pasta salad and drink wine to celebrate Adam's life.

"Where were you born?" Olivia asks, "You've never told me."

"I was born in Hollywood," I say. "Before everything went wrong. I was cradled in the Hollywood myth, the idea of showers of gold and sunshine. My father needed so many girls and my mother needed a guru and then another guru. California is the beginning and the end of the world."

"Sometimes I think we should move someplace else," Olivia says.

"Where would we go?" I say. "As we go to bed, as we get up, we're crunching on sunshine."

Olivia has brought tamales and Tallulah has brought her mother's cake. We eat and then we go outside to light candles for the dead and listen to music. Tallulah takes my hands, "Let the guilt go," she says, "be the love, be the river, be the river of love," and then the three of us take hands, and I am not alone.

CHAPTER 29

SEPTEMBER 4TH

When I clean Laura's house on Friday, September 4th, she has a girl there doing her nails. The girl is very beautiful with a long neck and hair down to her waist. While I'm cleaning the room, I ask her name and she says, "Dao. I worked in a nail salon, pre-pandemic," she says, "but of course, we closed and now the salon is all papered over, and they are seeing customers again on the sly."

"Why didn't you go back and be part of the sly?"

"Well, the owner really jacked the prices, and I didn't like that, so I just decided to go see some of my customers myself," she says. "I had just started at that salon, so I had brought my own customers."

While I clean the bunker, she gives Laura a massage and does her waxing. Altogether her services take about four hours. She says that most of her customers have her come every two to three weeks. I find out that Dao lives in Sherman Oaks in a guest house that one of her ex-boyfriends found for her. Dao seems to have dated some righteously rich guys, but she's still looking for the perfect man. She says that a lot of American men have the wrong idea about Asian women. They want an Asian woman who will be quiet and let them boss her around. "God, I say, I hope that had died with *Madame Butterfly*."

"Not at all," she says, "I've actually had men ask me if they can call me Lotus Blossom. I'm like Lotus Blossom my ass. I've been living in the US of A for twenty-five years and I speak better English than you do, yahoo, so no, say my name, bitch."

I start laughing. Laura has an eye mask over her eyes so she can rest, and she took some valium, though why she needs that, I don't know so I don't think she's really listening to this conversation. She gave me the money for Dao, before she got started and my own money as well, I guess in case she passed out. Dao finishes her nails and then Laura wakes up and goes to the fridge for a glass of ice and vodka. I get Dao's number and she goes out to her car and comes back shortly. "It won't start," she says.

Laura looks at the two of us. "You know you guys need to act like adults and take care of your vehicles," she says. She calls Triple A and they tow the car to Dao's mechanic near her house, but they won't give Dao a ride so I do. Dao is older than me and she's got some funny dating stories like the time a man asked her to dress up in a Chinese costume, "I'm Vietnamese," she had to explain, "and Vietnamese people do not traditionally love the Chinese."

"Oh," this guy says, "I thought you were Chinese. I was going to take you to Szechwan," or the guy who asked her, "I've heard that Asian women always put the man's pleasure first in the bedroom, is that correct? I just want to make sure. I am so looking forward to this."

And Dao said, "Oh yes, all Asian women exactly the same. First we pleasure man. Then we watch him fall asleep. Then we quickly slip out the door because we're so skinny; then we never come back or see his stupid face again. Sometimes we take wallet with us."

The guy was like, "What?"

She has me laughing all the way to her front door. "You are going to have to hang out with me and Olivia and Tallulah," I say. "We're going to hang out again soon, I'll let you know."

The next day, Laura's sister is having a party out at Yucaipa and Laura asks me to come to her house early to help her get ready. It's a Saturday and I'm already going to babysit Sheryl's kids in the afternoon, but I stop by and get her packed up and then drive to Sheryl's house. The twins are doing well. Sheryl and I have worked together and her therapist has been great. It almost makes me believe in therapy.

I've always had the feeling, since I left the cult that therapy might be an idea, but I know I can't afford it and I don't want to pay someone to know about my pain. It's my own to carry. It's my shame. If I tell anyone that my parents don't love me, that other person, that adult, is going to feel fucking sorry for me and I can't have that. I want to stand up for myself and create a life out of the smudge and drift of wretchedness I've been dealt and if I share this crap with anyone, that person will look at me, like you look at a fish when you lay it out and gut it. You see its head, its bones, its guts, its collar, its tail, its scales flaking off under your knife, and that will be me, that educated, smart therapist woman, I always picture a woman, arranging her glasses, sitting on her couch, beside her flowers and her artful art, and she'll say, "Mia, isn't that just terrible, tell me more." And she'll think as she drives away about me stripped to my underwear in front of Y, of me whipped, of me bruised, of me with my parents saying, "I don't want you. I don't want you. I don't want you. I don't want you." And she'll think, "That poor thing, she's a lost cause. She never had a chance. These creatures are bottom dwellers." She'll sip chardonnay with her husband, and she'll say, "I met this really pathetic creature today." Because the therapist will be in a higher class than me. So there's not a chance they can understand me.

But Sheryl's therapist is a miracle worker; she has Sheryl standing up to her boys; I may have to rethink therapy. She was a wheelbarrow of cray cray and look at her now.

We are making cookies when my phone rings, and Laura is so hysterical that I can't even hear her. "Slow down," I say. "I can't hear you."

"Turn on the news," she says. Sheryl turns on the news and there we see it. A huge fire bursting across Yucaipa County.

"Are you okay?" I say. I know they were going out there for a party, I can't remember the details. Her sister was having this party. Her sister is pregnant.

"It was a gender reveal party," she says. "For her baby, and we couldn't put out the fire."

"Wait," I say, "You guys started this fire?"

"My sister did. She lit fireworks for the party. We couldn't stop it. We did everything we could. Say something. I'm just calling you because I have to call someone."

"There are twenty-two massive fires going on in California right now," I say. "You have to hope no firefighters died in this fire. Why are you calling me? Why me?"

"I can't get a hold of Dao. I'm going to need a massage tomorrow," she says. "I'm really upset. See if you can call Dao."

When I call Dao, she says her car is going to cost twelve hundred to fix and she's grounded for now because she doesn't have the money. I call Laura back. She's driving.

"Look," she says. "Do whatever it takes. I am going to need to get a couple massages a week. This is way over the top."

"Dao's car is broken down and it's going to cost twelve hundred to fix, so she's not working until she can figure that out what to do."

"This is what you people do. You try to extort money out of rich people. I know what you're doing," Laura says, "And I won't be part of it."

"Good point," I say.

"Look," she says, "Can you come over and cook something for me and just hang out a bit until I can get some Xanax going? I can pay you a couple hundred dollars. My husband is no help. He doesn't listen to me. I'm so alone."

"Look at Waze, how long till you get home."

"Two and half hours."

"What if I meet you there, and get you settled and maybe I can drive Dao to your house this week. How's that."

"You are amazing. I've got some mushrooms for you, someone gave them to me today, I prefer pharm."

"See you later," I say.

When I arrive at the big house, she's disheveled and distraught. I get her settled in bed with a movie. "I only like movies from the eighties and nineties," she says. "I like *Backdraft*, I watch that movie a lot."

"You sure you don't want to watch *Look Who's Talking?*" I say.

"No," she says. "I need Kurt Russel."

"Okay then."

"Bring my wallet and bring the Xanax and bring some wine."

"Where is your husband?"

"He has a girlfriend; he thinks I don't know. He pretends to need to travel even during Covid. I hear him yelling at people on Zoom and I know he must be a beast to work with, but then I'll hear him cooing and sweet talking and I'll know it's her. She lives in Sherman Oaks. He's with her right now." She pops a couple Xanax and takes a gulp of wine. "Where would we be without pharm?"

"Lie back and rest," I say. She hands me some money and I don't count it. "I'll be back on Tuesday with Dao. I've texted her. I'll text you tomorrow."

"You're my best friend," she says. "I cannot live without you."

In the car, I reach into my wallet. She's given me five hundred dollars. "Lie back and rest," I say out loud, "the world is on fire."

CHAPTER 30

SEPTEMBER 12TH

DAO, OLIVIA, TALLULAH, LESLIE AND I are going out to the beach for a Saturday picnic. Dao fits right in with my friends. It turns out she was at several of the protests as well and she goes to the Pride march every year.

"Are you gay?" Olivia asks, ever the one to break the ice.

"No, I just believe in gay rights," Dao says. "Plus, let's be honest, there are no better parades than gay parades, just seeing those gays out there having a great time makes me weep with joy. I could be gay. I do like girls. I've just never had the guts to go through with it. It's hard to imagine calling my dad and telling him that I'm still a Buddhist but I'm a queer Buddhist now. I'm fine with guys. I mean they smell and they're kind of not that good in bed, but they're okay; my current boyfriend is not horrible."

"Wow, listen to yourself," Leslie says. "We should all be straight. I'm getting goosebumps. He's not horrible. You should get married right away if he's not horrible because about the best a man can do is not be horrible."

"Stop it," Dao laughs, "Maybe I do want to be with a woman." It's nice to be away from everything and to imagine this group as my posse. I figure people like Ed and Sheryl are only going to help me as long as I'm helping them, but these are my people. We stop on the way back at one of the farm stands to buy fruit. Olivia has a cousin who was picking fruit here. She got Covid, took two weeks off unpaid and then came back to work. Because everyone works closely together in the fields, the disease spreads even though they're working outdoors. Olivia wants to help her cousin get a job as a waitress and move into town, but now there are no restaurant jobs. We stop by to see her; she lives in a small trailer and her boyfriend opens the door. They come outside and we talk in the yard. Their baby isn't fat like Juan; he's skinny like he isn't getting enough to eat, and he cries all the time. I pick him up and he stops crying.

"He likes you," Olivia's cousin says.

"She's got the gift," Olivia says. "You should see her with Juan. He loves Mia. He puts his hands on her face and says, 'Mia Mia Mia.'" We laugh. I find myself wanting to give this couple whatever money I have, but I know that's the wrong thing to do. I'm a gringa and they're here working for themselves. What they want is more opportunities, not handouts.

"Hey," I say. "Do you guys have a car?"

"Yeah we do, but we just use it for groceries. We can walk to work. We take turns on the shifts because one of us has to look after Miguel."

"I'm getting requests for more house cleaning than me and Sophia can do. Do you want to try that?" I ask. "You could take Miguel along and put him in a playpen. They pay pretty decent. I have all these tutoring gigs now that are getting in the way and Sophia has tons of work. You'd think people would be worried about Covid, but white people don't want to clean their houses."

"I could do it," she says. "I've cleaned houses before."

"I'll go with you to the houses the first time," I say.

"And white people are always giving away stuff," Olivia says.

"Like what?"

"All kinds of stuff. Mama brings home food they didn't eat from parties and curtains they got rid of and so many clothes. White people have so many clothes it's unbelievable. How many clothes does a person need?"

"You need two sets of work clothes," I say, "and maybe one dress up and that's it. I think three outfits, a pair of flip flops, a pair of sneakers, you're good."

"These people have rooms for their clothing."

"No kidding," the cousin says. "Rooms?"

"You could lie down in these rooms where their clothing is and then let's talk about their bathrooms. Bathtubs like Jacuzzis right in their house."

"Your English is great," Dao says. "I've been here forever, and I still think English isn't easy."

Isabella smiles, "Community college," she says. "So, I gotta say, you're the first white girl I ever met who cleans houses. What happened to you?"

"It's a long story," I say.

"Her parents left her under a bridge," Olivia says, "And then my parents decided to adopt her, and we took her in, and she's my son's god mother."

"Were you like Moses in the basket?" Isabella says.

"She's kidding. I was not Moses in the basket. I keep telling her I was raised in a barn and born in a manger. But honestly, my parents didn't want me, so I ended up on my own. But now, this is my chosen family. Tallulah, Olivia, Leslie, her parents. Maybe Dao."

"Definitely me," Dao says.

"Very recently Dao," I say.

Isabella's boyfriend brings us all beers and we sit down on plastic chairs. The whole world is falling apart, and we are drinking beer in a circle of dirt in Ventura and making small plans. I want to be making large plans. I want to be changing the world. "What's that?" I ask pointing to a bird.

"European starling," Jorge says handing me another Dos Equis. "I'll tell you something about these birds. I've been studying up because local people seem to hate them. Look at him how confident he is." The starling with his fluffy black feathers looks from side to side like he owns the Valley. He has a jaunty look, like he's ready to go to a hot bar with a fast chick. One hundred birds were let loose in Central Park so that America could have all the birds of the Shakespearean world. This was in the 1890s. Now we have maybe two hundred million European starlings, and they are a menace to the North American bird world. People shoot them and poison them. Birders hate them. They take over nests of other birds. There are stories about these birds, that they'll leave their mate and find a second mate while their mate is raising young. Not often but they do, like a side dish. Often that side dish's young don't survive as well. Just like with humans. But what's interesting to me is that they were brought here and introduced to this environment, and now, people hate them. There are people who eat them. They only eat the breasts."

"Are we still talking about birds here?" I ask.

"I've seen white guys around here shooting them off the telephone wires with their shotguns," he says. "There's a lot of violence around here, and it's not just birds."

"Did you know a Black guy was lynched in the Antelope Valley?" Tallulah says.

"I thought he committed suicide," he says. "But whether he was lynched or not, it seems that he was being harassed by the Palmdale Peckerwoods. It's hard to believe that kind of racist gang is allowed to roam around, but this is America. I think they are still investigating whether it was a lynching, but even if it was not, what does it say about America, two Black men dead in ten days by suicide in Palmdale and Victorville. What is this country doing to people of color? It's okay to come here as long as you stay in your place. Mexicans and Salvadorans working in the fields are one thing, Black people walking around like they own this country, that is not something people are going to stand for."

On the way home I keep looking for starlings.

CHAPTER 31

SEPTEMBER 15TH

AT SOPHIA'S HOUSE WE ARE CELEBRATING Salvadoran
Independence day, although it's independence day for several Latin American countries. Sophia took the day off to
make pupusas and when I arrive, the house smells of food;
she's made tamales as well, and when I peek in the fridge, I
scream, "Dios!" She has made the tres leches cake. Hers is
unbelievable. I've brought a twenty-four pack of beer, so
they will have extra and I brought a sack of oranges. Juan
loves sucking on orange slices. Tallulah comes with me and
we both get to work setting the table outside.

I tell them that when I'm at different houses, people complain so much about their stock portfolios and not being able to
fly anywhere and not going to restaurants and not being able to
shop. But they still have me come over and clean the house.

"Americans are spoiled," Roberto says. "They always want
more, more, more. I think they fly around too much. One of
my bosses flies to New England once a year to look at the
leaves. Are you kidding me?"

"Maybe they really love leaves," I say. "Don't be judgy."

"You'd never hear El Salvadorans spending a couple thousand dollars going to Boston to look at leaves. If we had an extra two thousand dollars, we'd buy a better used car. I don't understand the stock market. It's invisible money. Rich people are propped up by invisible money, but poor people like us are propped up by nothing."

"That's not true," Tallulah says. Olivia brought out guacamole, chips and beer. "We're propped up by love. Look at us."

"Love doesn't pay the bills," he says.

"How important do you think love is?" Tallulah asks, drinking her Dos Equis. She reaches her hands to hold Juan. "Oh no you don't." He has a hand ready to reach into the guacamole.

"He had a face full of it earlier," Olivia says.

"I don't know," he says. "In the family, of course love is everything. But in society. What does love do? It doesn't keep cops from shooting people like us."

"But love is why we're here tonight," I say. "My parents didn't want me. But you wanted me as part of your family, and then you invited me here. Today I went to this house to tutor kids, and when I got there, the parents said they would pay me fifty dollars an hour to take the kids out of the house for four hours so they could have noisy sex. I took the kids to the park. When I came back, the parents were drinking champagne on the patio."

"I wonder if they were usually having the noisy sex while their kids went to school. The kids never leave the house. It's gotta be rough."

"Your neighbors have a sink and a toilet on their sidewalk," Tallulah says, "what's that about?"

"I think they're remodeling. When you go to Home Depot, there's a huge lineup of men buying supplies. Americans are nesting."

"I've been researching what Americans are doing," Tallulah says, "and I think a lot of us are crashing Pornhub, smoking weed, drinking a lot of booze and gaining weight, also a lot of binging on Netflix."

There's a knock at the door and since Olivia and Sophia are laying out food, I go to answer it with Juan in my arms. "Are we expecting a good-looking guy named Dan?" I ask.

"Bring him in, Mia," Olivia says. Dan has a large bouquet of tiger lilies and it's clear that he is in love with Olivia. He gives her a kiss in front of her parents and introduces himself as Olivia's boyfriend. We all get seated and I ask the big question.

"Okay, we're in the middle of a pandemic. Where did you two meet? You guys have some ninja skills."

"I'll say," Tallulah adds. "No offense," she nods at Sophia and Roberto, "but I haven't been laid for so long that I'm not sure I still know what to do, and look at you, with a baby, going out and getting you some, way to go girl!"

"We met at the park. She was there with Juan, and I was there with my dog, Champ."

"Is Champ a large guard dog?" Sophia asks. "Because now that we have a house, we've been talking about getting a guard dog." Olivia starts laughing. Juan in his highchair starts laughing too and banging his spoon although he may be just laughing along with his mother.

"Champ is a rescue dog, but mostly American Eskimo, so small and fluffy. I'll show you a picture later. She could guard a book or a paper airplane. We started meeting at the park, and I fell madly in love first with Olivia and then with Juan. It took Olivia a bit longer. She kept saying she couldn't fall in love with a white boy. And I kept saying I wasn't any white boy."

"What do you do?" Sophia asks.

"Please don't say you're a stock broker," Roberto says, "because we were just talking smack about the stock market."

"Or a cop," adds Sophia.

"Anything else I shouldn't do?" he asks.

"Let me see," Sophia says. "No lawyers, bankers, guys that work in finance, and absolutely no cops. No Marines. Hopefully nobody who works at a condom factory?"

"Why this list?" I ask. "I'm taking notes." I look at Olivia, "Did you know about this list?"

"Mama doesn't like anybody who's going to look down at us."

"We're making a lot of assumptions here," Dan says, "but you're in luck, I'm in med school. I'm planning to be a doctor. Are doctors okay?"

"Being a doctor has always been an honorable profession," Roberto says. Dan picks up the baby and carries him around the yard and comes back to the party. I see the parents watching him and I can see they're pleased. Olivia hasn't looked this happy in forever. It's odd that she and I are finding these smudges of happiness in the midst of a pandemic that is killing thousands of people and wiping out the world economy. Roberto turns on some music. He's started listening to more music in English and he likes PJ Harvey. "Down by the Water," rolls over the speakers.

"What do you think most white people are worried about?" he says.

"What they talk about is whether their kids will get into good schools, and whether they're getting fat, and whether their husbands are cheating, and how much money they've lost in the stock market, and sometimes the women talk about how their husbands can't get erections and how they can't get facials as often now and they miss flying around to different places."

"That's what I thought," he says. Dan is bouncing the baby on his knee and watching Roberto. He fits right in with our family. Sophia is moving to PJ Harvey's lyrics like she's been listening to this all her life. "The whole world is coming apart," Roberto says. "Because we live in a country where money is all that matters, and we have a president who only cares about money. Covid is the great equalizer. Maybe the president won't really notice unless he gets sick himself. We are supposed to be listening to the planet and listening to history. That's what Black Lives Matter is about in this country. We're inside history, and I'm afraid that with all the porn and food and booze, Americans are wasting the chance to wake up."

The music switches up to PJ Harvey singing with Nick Cave. I can't believe they're listening to this. This grinding dark sweet low music. I introduced them to this, but I didn't know how much they would love it. Tallulah lights a joint and passes it around and the smell unhinges the night. There's another knock and Leslie is here with a big basket of baked goods for the family. I didn't invite her, but Olivia did. She kisses me and takes the joint and I am folded into love. PJ Harvey's "When Under Ether" starts playing and Leslie and I are kissing.

"Let's sit down everybody and eat," Sophia says.

"Let's toast," Roberto says. We all grab a glass and Juan grabs his sippy cup. "This is to love, the kind of love that keeps us floating in the dark nights." Leslie has her arm wrapped around me; her hair is a little wet like she just showered, and she smells like night blooming jasmine.

CHAPTER 32

SEPTEMBER 18TH

I AM IN THE SWIMMING POOL with the twins when I hear my phone ring and I swim over to the edge. It's Ed. I still run his errands, but Frank does a lot more for him these days. "I'm so sorry, honey," he says, "Your hero is dead."

I comb through different people I've told him that I admire. "Wait," I say, "Not Ruth Bader Ginsberg. No, no."

"Yes," he says. "And that means that Trump will replace her immediately so he can make sure he has the Supreme Court he needs in case he needs to overturn the election." I climb out of the pool.

"I was just starting to hope that we would get rid of this guy. We can't survive another four years of this."

"What are you doing for dinner?"

"I don't know, I get off work at six."

"Come over. We need to catch up."

Sheryl's house is all red tile and palm trees and the slight smell of lavender. The pool is salt water, and I welter through the rest of the afternoon and make ice cream with the boys until she gets off Zoom and takes over and I take off for Ed's house.

Ed is a different man with Frank in his life and the house feels completely different. The heavy curtains are gone and have been replaced with shades, so the house has light pouring in. His backyard avocado trees have been pruned and now he always sends me home with some. The table is laid for dinner, and he has a bottle of wine out and open. Frank, Ed, and I step out on the patio with our glasses and toast. "Here's to Ruth," Ed says.

"Notorious," I say.

"And to the future," Ed says. "Whatever that might be." And at those words, I feel a crawling feeling at the back of my neck. "Let's go inside," he says.

We have appetizers. Shrimp cocktails. Something I mentioned liking once and here they are. Frank asks how my last semester at Pierce is going and when I'll be starting at UCLA, and I keep wondering why I feel like an egg is about to break. We have a salad and a whole baked fish which Frank cuts up onto our plates. It isn't until the dessert which is lemon sorbet and ginger cookies that Ed says, "I got a call from your father," and I say, "Say what? How did he have your number?"

And Ed says, "When I dropped you off that day, I gave my card."

"I see. What did he say?"

"He wants to talk with you."

"Why? I called him when my brother died, and he didn't give a shit."

"Things have changed."

"Like what?"

"His son died."

"He had another son?"

Ed takes a glass of limoncello and offers me some. I wave my hand. I can only drink so much and drive and I'm already considering spending the night. "Hold on. How old was the son?"

"Eleven, and he drowned in their pool. He wants to talk with you. I think he's in a lot of pain right now and I think you could try to see this from his point of view."

"What point of view?"

"Why don't you give him a call."

"Okay," I say. "I want to do the right thing." I look at Frank and I'm thinking Frank came back to his father, so maybe that is the right thing. Okay. Yeah. Everyone screws up.

I wake up at three in the morning and drive home. The next day, I call my father. A woman answers. "Hello, can I help you?"

"This is Mia, can I speak with Mr. Alexander."

"Look, he's not talking with his girlfriends," the woman says. "So, you can just leave him alone."

"I'm his daughter Mia," I say.

"Oh," she says, "of course, I knew you'd be calling, I just forgot your name. I'm so sorry, it's been so terrible. Can you come over? I can text you the address."

"Okay," I say.

I arrive back at the house in Bel Air. I feel nauseous as I knock on the door. The woman who opens is the woman who answered the phone. She introduces herself as Susie. She takes me to the backyard, and we sit on ornate patio furniture and music is playing from speakers overhead.

"I'm so glad to meet you," she says. She's pretty in a Los Angeles kind of way. She has the same nose everyone else has on television. From her tiny waist to her frozen face to her hair in pigtails, she looks like a tiny girl in a grown-up woman's house. It's very strange. The music is opera, I've heard enough at Ed's house to know that. I recognize the tune, but can't recall the name

"What are we listening to here?" I ask.

"My husband loves this. He can't get enough of Wagner. This is 'Ride of the Valkyries.'"

"What are they singing about?"

"They're ah, getting ready to take the dead bodies to Valhalla. That's their heaven," she says and I notice her eyes are glassy.

"What are you taking?" I say, "Atavan? Valium? Vicodin?"

"All of the above," she says. "I am underwater. He was swimming with his friends and we were in the bedroom having a fight because I found out he'd been cheating with all these girls. I don't even know how many. And one of the boys dunked him and we don't know because we weren't there and we haven't gotten a straight story, but the best story we've gotten is the boy held him down too long and when he came up, they all started trying to bring him back and they called us too late."

"I'm so sorry. I really am. I can't imagine what you're feeling."

"He hates me. He blames me. His first plan was to divorce me and marry Tiffany and have another son. I reminded him that Tiffany might be a gold digger and will take half his money. He's not in a position to drag through a divorce right now and there might be an easier way."

"Easier way to get what?"

"An heir. Which is why you are here."

"He is going to apologize and take you in. You are going to live here under our roof. We are going to pay for UCLA, and we are going to help you find a suitable husband and you can provide a grandchild. I think it will be good for you to be part of the family." We go inside and she pours me a glass of wine and we sit in the living room. The wine is deep red and the glass is almost full. She nearly spills it handing it to me. I don't know anything about wine, but this wine tastes good. The television is on in the background, and I can see Trump speaking at a rally in Minnesota. I can't hear him, but there is a sea of a MAGA hats. She sees me glance over. "We're big Trump supporters," she says. It's her first smile since I arrived. She's been speaking of her son, and her dead eyes haven't flickered, but when she mentions the leader, there's a bright spark. "What a man he is," she says. "You'll get to meet him too. We've had him for dinner right here at the house." She smiles girlishly and shakes her head and those little pigtails wiggle. "I think he likes me. He said I should sit on his lap."

"Susie," I say. "I'm not even sure I like boys. I've never even kissed a boy."

"You'll like boys just fine. No one really likes kissing boys. I mean come on. Men are mean. You just close your eyes and bear it."

"I'm pretty sure there are men and women who love each other," I say. "My friends Sophia and Roberto adore each other."

"Where are they from?"

"El Salvador, why?"

"People from El Salvador aren't the same as us."

"I don't follow you at all."

"You're wrong about so many things," Susie says. "We need to take over your upbringing before it's too late. You're staying for dinner. We're ordering from Wolfgang Puck."

My father enters from his upstairs office. He seems inebriated and he says hello to me briefly. There's a knock on the door and Susie tells me to please go answer. At the door there's a young man in a suit who introduces himself as Brad. Susie says she and my father need to freshen up and dinner will be served in a half hour, and Brad and I can get to know each other. I take Brad outside as far away from the house as possible, so we aren't spied on. "Brad, why are you here tonight?"

"To meet you," he says. "Your father wants us to get married."

"How do you feel about this," I ask.

"I want my father to be proud of me. I work in finance, and I guess, I could use a wife at company parties and so on, and I'm not likely to find one because I'm gay."

"Well, so am I."

"Maybe this could work out."

"Why would we live a lie for our parents in 2020?"

"So, they leave us a lot of money?"

"Right, let me think, I live a miserable life with someone I neither know or like and pretend to be someone I'm not so I can have money. Sounds stupid."

"Where do you live now?"

"In a yurt."

"This would be a terrific step up for you and all you have to do is pretend to be straight and next thing you know you'll have a decent haircut, a manicure and pedicure, you'll be shopping at Saks, which from the look of your clothes would be a big step up and I can tell you from talking with girls, you'll get used to comfort pretty quickly. It's time to change your life. Come on, being married to me wouldn't be that bad. I'm easy going. You just have to shop and make babies."

We walk around the yard which is full of sunflowers and bougainvillea. I keep thinking that in a moment your life can change. I could become a mother. I could see Leslie on the side and Brad could see his lovers on the side. How many times would we have to do it to get a baby? Probably once or twice. We're back in the house and my father sits down at the head of the table. The MAGA rally is still going on in the background.

"Trump's a great man," my father says. "Best president we've ever had. He's putting everyone in their place." His face is blotchy and I wonder if it's tears or alcohol.

"Who do you hang out with?" Brad says.

"I have some great friends," I say glad the conversation is turning from the president for the moment. "I have a couple friends from school, Tallulah and Olivia, we hang out a lot and I have a new friend Dao."

"This is going to end," my father says. "We'll find you some new friends. You need to hang out with your own kind. You won't learn anything hanging out with people who are just barely hanging on. They're trying to get handouts. They convinced my friend Royal to buy them a house because they were too lazy to buy their own house. I can't have you hanging out with them, and the Black girl is lucky she didn't get arrested. Don't worry. We'll get you all prettied up; you'll make new friends at UCLA. You can join a sorority." My father puts his hand on my shoulder. I feel like a lost girl who is found and taken in. "You're part of this family now;" he says, "we're a great family." He's staring at me, and I realize that he's drunk and suddenly I feel a switch go off in my head.

"Mama said that you guys had a terrible marriage," I say. "She said that you screamed at her all the time, that you belittled her and called her a cunt, and finally she took us and ran off and joined the cult and you never came after her to see the kids until you decided to see Adam and when you realized he was queer, you didn't want him. And if you'd known I was queer as well, I wouldn't be sitting here, so let's just admit, that this family, like this country was never great, was never exceptional was always flawed. America is a country where the bullies win. This is me saying goodbye. Goodnight Brad, Goodnight Susie, Goodnight Father. Be safe and be well."

"I will never offer to provide for you again."

"I am sorry about your loss." The door closes with a thud, and I hear Susie crying and my father screaming at her to shut the fuck up. Stepping outside into the night air feels like the best thing I've done for myself in a long time. I can't believe I thought for even thirty seconds about marrying

Brad. What a name. Being married to Brad and having tea at the Beverly Hilton seems like a fate worse than death. I don't know what I will say to Ed. I hope he won't be disappointed in me, but seriously, what would he have me to do? I drive home in the dark and as I near my yurt, I see a deer standing in the street as if she's watching over me, as if she is waiting for me to come home.

CHAPTER 33

SEPTEMBER 21ST

THE PANDEMIC MOVES ON SLOWLY. ON the West Coast, we mask in public. But, I am too poor to not take risks. My life is a risk. I don't think about the virus all the time. When I go to people's houses, they watch the news. I have no news to watch.

All weekend I don't hear from Ed, and on Monday, I pull up at Laura's house and knock. Her husband answers the door. "You're back," I say.

"Come in," I follow him inside and he pours me a cup of coffee. "Cream?"

"Sure," I say.

"Did she say where I had gone?"

"Where is she?"

"She's upstairs, still asleep, too much Valium. So?"

"She said you were with your girlfriend."

"I see."

"Not my business at all. I'm just here to clean the house. I have no opinions," I say starting to clean the kitchen.

"Well, that's a good thing," he says, "because you are not entitled to any opinions here. Nor do I give a shit what you think." I don't say anything. I start polishing the furniture in the living room overlooking the pool, but he follows me. "She was fun for one maybe two years, and the thing about the film industry is you meet a lot of cuties. You don't see these movie stars settling down, that's because there's a lot hot pussy floating around, and she's floating on a sea of pharm. I give her a life, but now that Covid has hit, she's just going bonkers."

"Do I need to clean the bunker?"

"No, we haven't been out there," he says. "You're the kind of girl that if you were in the film industry, you would get nowhere. You don't have a breathless voice. You sound like you're thinking all the time. You don't have big tits. Tell me what's the most expensive clothing store you've ever been to."

"Buffalo Exchange? I went into a Macy's once but I couldn't afford anything."

"Not even Nordstrom?

"No."

"H&M? Their stuff is cheap."

"No, I don't need clothes. I only have two outfits."

"Oh, good lord, no, that would not work. You have to care about how you present yourself, you have to be a narcissist to make it in Hollywood. Aren't all Gen Zers narcissists?"

"Wow, you are generalizing a personality type for an entire generation, that's crazy and no. And I'm talking to a man who owns a Ferrari and a Maserati."

"Tell me an adventure you've had."

"I was getting away from the place where I grew up; it had become dangerous. I had been in San Francisco, and then I hitched out of the city, and this woman dropped me by a pond outside of Marin. I didn't have much with me, but I set up camp and slept in my sleeping bag. When I woke, I was hungry, and I had no food, but the pond had all these frogs, and I got it in my head that I was going to eat frogs' legs. I'd heard of people eating them. But no one had explained how many frogs you had to kill to get enough to eat or how long it would take, plus there was the actual killing of the frogs."

"What do you do?"

"Well, you bang the frogs on the head. I killed three frogs, and I got a fire going and cooked the little legs and it was sickening thinking how recently those legs had been hopping and swimming around that very pond. I wasn't going to last long by that pond with my small knife and fry pan. That's what adventures are like for me, you're hungry, and you're sitting at a campfire with a pile of bloody frog bones and guts picking away at tiny legs."

"What a story," he says. "What a trash life you've lived. I wish you a great life."

One that doesn't end up with me being fired, I think. *I've always wanted a yellow brick road. This guy wants to cliff dive. That's because he's never seen the bodies at the bottom like I have or heard the screams of all of us falling.*

I keep cleaning, and he keeps talking. "In Hollywood, that's everything. That's why I bought this house."

"Correct me if I'm wrong, but isn't this house in the wrong part of town? Aren't you supposed to be in Malibu or the Hollywood Hills? Why Granada Hills, this is where people accidentally end up when they're driving in circles in the Valley and they can't figure out how to get on the Five freeway. They say to themselves, 'Where the fuck am I?' and they get on the Five and get the fuck out of here. I'm just saying. Your house is fancy and all, but it's nowhere."

"That's what I said when we were building it," Laura says coming into the living room behind me with a cup of coffee. "I was like, we're going to live where?"

"Film people live everywhere at this point because you fly everywhere," he says. "What are you in college for? My wife tells me you plan to go to UCLA. I went there for film school."

"I think I'm going to be a writer."

"Good choice," he says, "then you can always be ridiculous, poor, have bad taste, and think you know so much more than you actually do. Writers get little bits of information which they digest and spit out in their books, but they never live anything, partly because they can't afford to go anywhere or do anything, and partly because they're scared as mice, but mostly because most writers don't have the emotional ability to float their own boat. They are always capsizing, and that process of capsizing takes up all their time, poor little lunatics."

"Stop talking to her that way!" Laura says taking a pineapple out of the fridge and beginning to slice it. "Come on, Mia, let's have some pineapple. She's my only friend."

"Oh yes," he says. "Roger that, the help is your only friend. You know when you make a movie, millions of people see it, so that story is spun out and you influence the zeitgeist. When you write a book, if you're lucky maybe a few thousand read it, and if it's a poetry book, maybe a few hundred, and that's what makes writers so crazy, they know what they're doing is like whispering fairytales to a group of mad children in the forest. You can do it, but if you stop doing it, no one really cares."

"Donald, stop it," Laura says. "Get out of here, let us eat our breakfast in peace."

"You know the joke about writers?" he asks.

"No," I say.

"Well, they're making this war movie, and this blond woman with big tits wants a part, so she gets to the set and she meets the writer and she goes and sleeps with him and he gets her a part, and she's walking along in the mud behind the cavalry, rain pouring down on her and she says, 'Who do I have to fuck to get out of this movie?' and the point is," but I cut him off.

"I get the point. The writer is powerless. But words are powerful."

"Not when they come from someone who looks like you do."

"Donald, get the fuck out of here." We hear the Maserati exiting the garage with a roar, and she goes out to lie by the pool with some coffee and liquid Vicodin. "That's the sound of his penis exploding," she says. "I wish. Mia," she says, "Get Dao to come over and give me a massage. I'm really having a tough time. I've sent the kids to boarding school, and it's just fraying my nerves. I just don't know if I can get through all this."

I call Dao and she arrives and gives Laura a massage. "Can you order lunch for all of us? Order us some Thai food. I just need something to calm my nerves." Dao orders the food, and we sit down to eat with Laura. "I like food that requires chopsticks," she says. "I'm very good with them." We can see the drugs are kicking in. "I think you two should come every day."

"Laura," I say. "You have us coming twice a week now, maybe that's enough?"

"You know the fire my sister caused? Well, a fireman died. And I'm worried that my sister could get charged with man-slaughter. You two need to come at least three days a week, I can't manage otherwise."

"I'm so sorry," I say. "That's brutal. Let us talk a bit and I'll text you."

"I can't be alone so much. I get so lonely in between you guys coming." she says. "Can I call you guys? When I'm lonely and I want to talk? He's out fucking whatshername."

"Sure," I say, "Give me a call."

"I think the three of us should go for a swim," she says. By the time we have cleaned up from lunch, she is passed out. We carry her upstairs, set the alarm, and leave.

As we leave, Dao remarks, "Rich people don't have everything."

"I keep worrying that we'll find her dead of an overdose," I say.

My phone rings and it's Ed. "Why don't you come over," he says. "I'd like to hear what happened."

WHEN I'VE TOLD ED WHAT HAPPENED at my father's, he sits quietly for a moment and then he gets up and walks out into his garden. The lavender is growing, sprays of purple along the fence. He comes back to where I'm sitting at the patio table. "Back to zero," he says.

"There's no back to zero," I say. "I've always had zero family except Sophia and Roberto and they can't do anything for me. I'm right where I always was. No one to disappoint. No one to impress."

"No one to build a foundation for you. No one to help you find your way."

"And who is to say there's anything wrong with wandering in the dark? The Children of Israel wandered for forty years, and they found Canaan."

"That's a terrible example considering the wars in the Middle East."

"Wandering is a special kind of joy."

"Do you want to be the kind of second-class citizen who eats at Denny's and stays at crappy motels with ratty bedding and goes to college at state schools and wears clothes that look like you got them in a dumpster? You could have been an upper-class person."

"Ah, now we get to it. I'm not acting like an upper-class person. I've never stayed at any motels or eaten at Denny's and yes, I'll be delighted to go to UCLA and yes, my clothes look like shit." I'm wearing cutoff jeans and a tank top. "But to be my father's daughter, I was going to have to wear a MAGA hat and become someone I'm not."

"Couldn't you just lie?"

"If you lie long enough, you become someone you don't recognize in the mirror. I'm sorry if you've lost your faith in me."

Frank opens the door and comes out. "How's our little rebel?" he says.

"I said no to wearing a MAGA hat."

"You know, not everyone looks good in them. Dad, let her be herself. It's all she's got." He walks me to my car. "He'll come around," he says. "Give him time." He hands me a bag of oranges. "Never lose your juice," he says.

I call Leslie on the way home. "What you got going?" she says.

"I got juice," I say.

"I'm coming your way," she says. "See you on the flip side."

CHAPTER 34

NOVEMBER 3RD

SALLY CALLS ME ON THE WEEKEND to confirm that Sophia and I are going to clean the house on Election Day because she and Chuck are throwing an Election Day party. They've invited fifty people over for a celebration. Even for me, going house to house, I think this is a bit much. I wear a mask at people's houses. This party will clearly be unmasked. Since Sally has started watching Fox News, she's gone over to Chuck's way of thinking about a lot more things. She tells me that she really enjoys Fox News; at first the little Foxers amused her with their stories which seemed too farfetched to be true, but the more she watches, the more she can't bear a day without the little Foxers, who from Tucker to Hannity can take any story and spin it like a top. But she likes their spin; she likes their version.

"I like to see things from both sides," she tells me. But she doesn't; she only likes the Fox side.

"I use my tiny income for a student digital subscription to *The Economist* and *The New York Times*," I say. "One is centrist, one is liberal. Fox is lying to old people. You shouldn't be watching it."

"I'm not old," she says. "A lot of people think I'm in my thirties."

Oddly almost everyone I clean houses for has asked me at one time or other how old they appear to be. I've learned to never answer this honestly. The fact is even with Botox, there is something in our eyes that ages us. Our eyes and our hands betray us, and for some of us our gestures and posture as well. Sally is slender, dark haired, green eyed and tall, but she looks like she's in her fifties even though she exercises like a demon.

"Tell me about the party," I say.

"Well, it's going to be all Trump supporters, so we want to serve food Trump would eat."

"But he's not coming, you should have food you like to eat."

"But we're celebrating how much we love Trump," Sally says.

"Okay, so fast food then?"

"You bet, we are ordering a bunch of hamburgers from McDonalds and fries and lots of Diet Coke, you know he drinks like ten of them a day, and we'll have a bucket of KFC."

"This is California. Most people like to eat healthy; do you think people will eat all this?"

"What's not healthy about this? Everyone's excited. I've let them know that we're going to have Trump food delivered."

"But wait, you shouldn't drink any alcohol or smoke weed. Trump doesn't drink and I think we should assume he doesn't eat apples or make apples into bongs." I know that Chuck and Sally love their bongs. When I clean up their house, it's here a bong, there a bong. I've found roach clips in the bedroom, in the bathroom, in the kitchen, the TV room, and in the man cave.

"Well, we're going to drink anyway, and you know we're going to hot box the house," she laughs.

"We will be there to get the house cleaned up spick-and-span for your MAGA delights," I say.

ON THE DRIVE OVER, I GET on the phone with Dao. "Hey Dao," I say, "You know how we always hear clients say, 'I can't go to Home Depot anymore, because their founder is supporting Trump,' or 'I can't buy In-N-Out any more, the owners support Trump.'"

"Yeah, I always hear that. I take note of it. Why do you ask?"

"Well, we take money from Trump supporters. Is that dirty money?"

"Yes, it's filthy money once it's been in their little Trumper hands, and we take it and clean it up. We're too poor to only take blue money; we must take the red money and make it blue."

"Are you sure it works like that?"

"Does for me. Are you working for some dirty Trumpers today?"

"Don't say it like that, but yes."

"On Election Day?"

"They're having this massive party."

"You want to come to my apartment afterward? You can watch the results, and we'll turn your money to good use and get a pizza. Invite Leslie too. I like her."

"I'm there," I say.

WHEN I SHOW UP AT DAO'S place, Leslie is already there, and they are both doing their nails. "How'd it go?" Dao asks.

"Well, it was just them there, and they are really hoping Trump will win. The house is all decorated with MAGA stuff. We got out before their friends arrived." Dao has a cute place in Sherman Oaks with a little balcony. She's got some nice beer ready for us to watch the results pour in. Leslie brought ice cream and fruit.

We start hopping from one channel to the next eating bites of our pizza. Dao starts declaring that we will leave the country if Trump gets elected, and I say I'll go too, but none of us are clear on where we'll go or with what money. When Florida and Texas go to Trump, we stop eating and drinking. We can't think or breathe. We go to Rachel Maddow and she's giving us some hope, but this is what happened last time, and we can't live through this again. Then, at some moment when Dao is flipping around, she lands on Fox News for a minute, and they call Arizona for Biden, and I'm like, "Fuck, this is happening. Fox just called Arizona for Biden," and at this point, we can see the map. We can see the uncounted states, and we can see that we have a fighting chance. The blue wall is building and it's like that moment when you're in a car crash or about to be in one, and you know your car is small and you will die and then the tractor trailer swerves and you feel your adrenaline shooting through your body like you were on fire, and suddenly the road is up ahead of you and you're going to live. That's how I felt when Arizona is called for Biden. We're going to live.

The next few days are a muddle. It is hard to work watching the news and going to take care of the kids, but Saturday morning, we all meet at Sophia's house, and she's made tamales to celebrate what we hope will be the victory. She runs a cord out into the yard and hooks up the TV, and we all watch Biden and Harris speak and then the streets of DC run sticky with champagne. New York City is like joy turned on; you see people dancing everywhere, in Brooklyn, in Central Park, in Bryant Park. All over the world, people breathe, as if a tyrant has left the room and we no longer have to feel afraid. Leslie, Tallulah, Olivia, Dan, Dao and I start dancing, and then Leslie and I start kissing, and I begin to think that it isn't the end of the world after all. I begin to think, I may get to 2021, and when I get there, maybe I'll be dancing.

"Get a room," Olivia says laughing. But she and Dan are kissing too.

"Oh, I'm going home with her," Leslie says.

"It's not much of a room," I say.

"You're there," she says, "it's a great room."

CHAPTER 35

NOVEMBER 28TH

LESLIE OPENS THE WINDOW OF THE yurt early Saturday morning. I stand beside her in my tank top and underwear. Outside the yurt is a deer. She's looking at us and with her is a half-grown fawn. We don't move, and finally she moves away, her tail in the air, her fawn following gracefully. It's the weekend before Thanksgiving. I'm cleaning houses Monday with Sophia, but then we're all getting Covid tests and we're not going anywhere until the holiday. I've taken to getting Covid tests every week, and Sophia and her family do too. We are essential workers of a kind, and Sophia and her daughter both have Diabetes Type One, so I worry about them. We wear gloves and masks when we go to people's houses, but the people don't, and I don't want any of us to get sick but especially not Sophia. I can't make any food for the holiday, but I have promised to bring the beer, so I'm bringing pilsner beer and Tecate. My phone rings, and I look at it thinking it must be a mistake. It's Mrs. Royal.

"Hello," I say, thinking this must be a wrong number. She's crying so hard that I can't understand anything at first. She keeps talking fast and loose, but I have no idea what she's saying, and finally I cut in and say, "Mrs. Royal, do you want me to call for help? Do you need help?"

She says, "You come help me. I'll pay you. Come, please." I've never heard her say, "please," so I jump in my car and drive over there. I have an evening childcare job, but nothing until then. I was going to try to learn yoga, but I can do that another time.

I get to the Royals, and I get ready to ring the bell, but I decide to try the door first. It's unlocked. I open it and call, "Mrs. Royal!" No answer. Inside, the whole place smells strange. Their small dog hasn't been let out. I let him out into the backyard and clean up the kitchen floor and then go upstairs. I knock on the master bedroom door, and there's a muffled sound inside that sounds like, "Come in."

I open the door a crack, "Do you want me to come in?"

"Yes, please, that's why I called you. I need help."

She's in bed; the shades are pulled and there's a pile of tissues beside her. "Are you sick? Do you want me to call your doctor?"

"No," she says. I've never seen her without makeup and surprisingly she looks younger and better, but her hair is a mop. "He left me for a bunny."

"Mrs. Royal," I say, "There aren't Playboy bunnies any-more. The magazine closed down."

"She was in the magazine a few years ago. How can I compete with that? Her tits are like a foot above mine. Her ass is probably two feet above mine. I met her; at a party we were at, and we had a conversation with her, and she said, and I quote, 'I like to read *Calvin and Hobbes* and I like Barbie dolls and I like watching the Kardashians.' She has no brains in her little head, and he's leaving me for her? I can't believe it. I thought we were an epic couple. I don't know how to do anything. He was always here at night. He blew out the candles. The night he left, they just kept burning, and I didn't know what to do. I watched them burn and I drank a lot of wine."

"Okay, how long ago was this? How long have you been in the house alone?"

"What day is it?"

"Saturday."

"Three days."

"Why me? You treat my family like shit, and then you fire me. Why me?"

"I can't have any friends know what's happening."

"Where are the rest of your helpers?"

"They talk too much."

"Got it. I'm nobody. Okay, so let's get you downstairs and get you some coffee." She has a cappuccino machine and I get that going and make her a large one, and then I make the bed and clean the bedroom and bathroom and feed the dog. "Do you have any family members you could go to?"

"I don't think so," she says. Her face is still a blur. "Look," she says, "I was rotten to you and your friends. It was nice of you to come."

"Look," I say. "I think this is a hard time for you to be alone. I think if you had company, someone you have fun with, you could start to make plans for the future. Do you have any girlfriends you trust?"

"Not really," she says. "No one who would come over and stay with me." I am remembering the questions we learned in psych class to ask to find out if someone is suicidal, but I'm not sure if that's what's going on here.

"How do you feel when you're alone?" I ask.

"Like I want to die," she says. "What makes a woman whole is having a husband. A married life is a party; it has structure and plans. A single life is like a worm squiggling on the pavement. It might get run over. It doesn't matter."

"Wow," I say. "On behalf of all of us single people who are loving and living our single lives to the full, waking up every day and doing whatever the fuck we want to without having to ask someone's permission, fuck your worm analogy." She laughs.

"Fuck your worm analogy? Okay, I'm just not used to this yet."

"Let me show you your future. You are beautiful and full of life. You have learned a new compassion for others which makes you a better person and a better friend. You get a lawyer, and you get a divorce. You keep the house. You figure out what you like to do. What you want for dinner. Where you want to travel. What have you ever wanted out of life that Mr. Royal stopped you from doing?"

"I want to study art," she says. "He says it's stupid and people will laugh at me."

"Do it, where do you want to study?"

"Otis, I want to study painting there, if I can get in. I used to be an artist and I want to be one again."

"Well, why don't you just do it. He's gone. It's time to claim your story."

She gets a bath while I clean the house, and I make some chicken soup and have it simmering for her. I set up some groceries to be delivered the next day and I tell her I can come by on Monday to check on her.

When I come by Monday, she says, "What am I going to do for Thanksgiving?"

"I don't know," I say. "Do you want me to set up dinner delivery?"

"I want to come spend Thanksgiving with you or have you come over here," she says. "We could watch TV."

"Mrs. Royal," I say.

"Please call me Joy," she says.

"Joy," I say. "I am going to be with Sophia, Roberto, Olivia and Olivia's son, Juan, and a few friends. We are having El Salvadoran food, tamales, and we are having turkey and cranberries, and we are all getting Covid tests before we come."

"Can I come?"

"I have to ask Sophia," I say. "And you would need to be nice and have a Covid test."

WE HAVE BEEN CLEANING THE HOUSE all day and we have the best china and napkins on the picnic tables in the back-yard where Roberto has strung fairy lights. The turkey is done at 4 p.m. and the Rolls purrs into the driveway and Joy gets out with a bag of champagne, chocolate, and a magnificent apple pie. She immediately walks up to Olivia and apologizes. "Olivia, I'm sorry we didn't stand up for you. We were cowards. We were wrong."

Olivia who has been doing breathing exercises all afternoon puts out her hand, and while they are shaking hands, Juan runs up and says, "Is the chocolate for me?"

Joy apologizes again to the whole family for her son, her husband, and herself. They give her a glass of Tecate and I can tell she's never had it, but she drinks it with gusto and Juan smiles at her with his little dimples, she hands him a toy car, and he climbs into her lap like he's known her all his life.

We sit down and Roberto says the blessing and we begin the turkey, the tamales, the cranberry, the stuffing, the makings of an American and Salvadoran mixed up dinner, and afterward, when we're cleaning up, Roberto starts playing the guitar and Joy is dancing with the baby in her arms under the lights. She's got stained cranberry from Juan's hands on her dress, but she clearly doesn't care. When we're finished, we come out, and we watch them dance, and she comes over to hug me goodbye and thanks Sophia for everything, and that night everything seems perfect.

Before I go to sleep at night, I try to keep from doom-scrolling and instead, I write in my journal and read a bit. The moon overhead is sliced, but it glows. There's a vulture hanging around Sophia's house, and I cannot shake the idea that he knows something.

CHAPTER 36

DECEMBER 24TH

BY CHRISTMAS, IT SEEMS LIKE EVERYONE in Los Angeles has had Covid. When New York City was drifting with coronavirus in April, it seemed so clear, a city where people lived smashed together in apartment buildings, a city where people spend so much time in subways and taxis, a city where people run into each other at bars and restaurants. In Los Angeles, you never run into anybody at all. You make an appointment to go to their house, because you don't want to drive an hour and find them not there. Los Angeles is a sprawl city, but of the ten million of us who live here, many of us don't live in houses; many of us are crowded into apartments which are cesspools of Covid. Thanksgiving parties, holiday parties, it's all catching up on us. I am wearing a mask as I jump from house to house, but my employers expect me to show up. I've stepped up my testing to twice a week, and I tell myself, what if I worked at a hospital or a grocery store?

Every house I go to, the news is on all the time, some people running CNN, or the regular news if its evening, and of course, Chuck and Sally are always listening to the Foxers gossiping amongst themselves. This is only the second election I've really been aware of, and it's breathtaking to me that we've had a legal election and the president is trying to overthrow it. In our Civics class, our professor has explained the Constitution and he says that the checks and balances will keep him in check, but it's clear that a lot hangs on what shenanigans he comes up with on January 6th. I don't understand how the 45th even is getting away with this and nobody is really explaining it.

Leslie and I are hanging together a lot, but I get the feeling she wants me to move out of the yurt, she doesn't think it's safe. I tell her that when I sleep in the yurt, the moon is following me at night because I can see it, and she tells me that's not enough of a reason to live anywhere. She also likes to ask me what I'm going to do besides write. She means a real job with real income. The great thing about having no parents is having no one to disappoint and no one to please. No one expects anything of me, but now, Leslie seems to. The thing is I haven't gotten much further than a college education free of debt and then I want to write. The job part is what grown-ups do and that still seems far away. I can picture still living in the yurt for a few years doing what I'm doing, but she says when I graduate, I should have a plan. We make a list of things I like to do to see if that helps: hiking, sleeping, drinking tea, dancing. None of it is adding up to a job.

Christmas Eve, she and I go to over to Sophia's house and we help make tamales and drink beer. Juan stays up late and eats some cooked masa. Sophia and Roberto love having a house and Olivia has painted Juan's room like a jungle. I've brought him a Piglet which he kisses. When we get the tamales done, we clean up, light candles, and lay the table for dinner, but Sophia says she wants to lie down. Roberto says not to worry, she's probably just tired, she always gets up too early Christmas morning.

But on Christmas Day, he calls me early and asks me to come. He doesn't say why, and I don't ask. They've already called the doctor, and they've said not to bring her to the hospital unless she's turning blue or can't breathe. Roberto is a good man, but Sophia has taken care of him in their married life and Olivia is with the baby. I arrive and double mask, put on gloves and clean the bathroom from where she was sick in the night. She's pouring sweat, and I change the sheets and wash them. I'm not going to work for ten days because I'm exposed, so I buckle in. They don't have regular medical insurance, just La Clinica, and those are full, so we do everything we can for Sophia. When Roberto gets sick too, Olivia and I are working double shifts at the house, and she tries to keep the baby out of the way.

We call 911 three days later, and they are both taken to Olive View. We wait and pray and hope for the best. We feel sure they will survive. We can barely eat or sleep and no one can visit us. Leslie calls every day. Dao drops off food, and we manage to eat the Thai lemongrass soup. She knows us well. Dan calls every day. Sophia and Roberto both die on New Year's Eve as the fireworks start in our neighborhood. Olivia cries as though she cannot stop. I hold her. I feed the baby. I cannot breathe.

I get on the phone with the hospital and make the arrangements and get her to come on and say yes. We pick up the urns with their ashes on January 5th and invite over Tallulah, Leslie, Dan, and Dao for a funeral in the backyard. Leslie asks if they had left a will, and Olivia says, "Yes, as soon as Covid started, my mother insisted, and then she revised it after the Royals left us this house. I think the house was left to them and me, but I don't even know. My mother keeps her documents in her dresser, I'll go get it."

She comes back with two handwritten pieces of paper. "Each of them wrote the same thing it looks like," she says. She hands it to me, "You read it."

"Well," I say, reading it, "this is very odd. Olivia, they've left you their money and bank accounts and your mother left you all the contents of the house and her personal effects, but she and Roberto left their part of the house to me, and they said they hoped I would come and live with you and help you with Juan. But look, you might want to be alone."

Olivia looks at me suddenly wide eyed. "They're leaving you their part of the house? So you have to come stay with me and be my roommate? And I won't be alone? Oh my God—God loves me. We can be sisters."

"I'm ready," I say, "let's light a candle for them." Dan is so sweet, he has his arm around her, but clearly, he knows that it would be rushing her for him to move in on her.

She asks me and Leslie to stay the night, and we ask about Dan. "We've just started," she says. "We're not intimate yet. We have time. No pressure. I want to just take my time. I want you to come over whenever you want though, Leslie."

Leslie and I sleep in the living room on the couch and sometime in the night, Juan climbs out of his bed and joins me on my couch. "Mia," he says, "stay with me," and I do.

THE NEXT DAY, I'M AT CHUCK and Sally's cleaning the house. When I arrive, the house has a beat to it. They're listening to music I haven't heard before, and it takes me a minute and then I say, "Is this Elvis?"

"You're a little young for to know Elvis," Chuck says.

"I heard him a couple times, and that voice is unmistakable. What's he singing?"

"He's singing 'Dixie,'" Chuck says, and I hear the wail to look away. I start my work, and I want to look up the lyrics of this song. What are we looking away from?

"Isn't this the song of the Confederacy?" I ask.

"It celebrates the South," he says, "And I'm Southern. You got a problem with that?"

"God bless America," I say. But my stomach is sick.

Sally expresses her condolences about the death of my friends. She says, "I'm sorry about Sophia," and she pats me on the shoulder.

"Why did they die?" Chuck asks. "I know people eighty-five years old that recovered from Covid, of course they weren't overweight. Fat people who get Covid die and the reason so many Black and Mexican people die is because they're fat. Sophia had a few pounds on her." I stop cleaning then. My friend Sophia was medium height and build, about a size twelve, a round little lady, who cleaned this man's toilets.

"That's racist," I say. "Black and Mexican people have frontline jobs which is why so many of us who are people of color are getting Covid. There are plenty of overweight White Americans and I can't have you smack talking my friend who just died. I won't stand for it." I can feel a ringing in my ears. I look down at my hands which are shaking.

He pauses. I'm in a barely controlled rage. Sally comes into the kitchen. "What's happening here?" she says.

"She just called me a racist."

Sally looks at me. "I need you to apologize or get out," she says.

"Understood," I say. I grab my bag and go. In my car, I start crying, tears of rage and horror. I wonder if he's still listening to "Dixie." I feel trampled underfoot.

As I DRIVE AWAY, I FIGURE out if I'm going to make it on the bills this month without this job. I will of course, I just won't save as much toward UCLA. Would it have hurt me to apologize? It has been days, only days, since we dug a hole in the backyard, buried the ashes and planted a red Salvadoran orchid and Olivia sang to her mother, and we all wrote a goodbye note. I may still have ashes on my fingers.

When they tell us in our class on race and privilege, when to fight, when to be an ally, when to give in and compromise, it isn't a choice of feeding the baby or not. It's always a philosophical choice. If I had parents, they would have explained all this to me, given me a moral compass. I drive to the ocean since I have the day off, and I take a walk on the beach. What I learn from that walk is that if this was a mistake, I'll figure that out, but right now, it feels good. I couldn't stand in that kitchen another moment. I stood up for the living and the dead, and if we don't stand up for our tribe, then we don't have one.

CHAPTER 37

JANUARY 6TH

SOME PEOPLE JUST TAKE UP SPACE on the planet, and when they die, they're gone but no one misses them very much. Sophia was no smudge of air. I feel like I can't breathe without her in my life, and somehow it is so right that Olivia and I are mourning together. We bump into each other crying, morning and night and in the middle of the night. Leslie is at the house a few nights a week, Dan comes over on weekends, and Dao and Tallulah are all checking on us. Leslie comes on Tuesday to spend the night and we wake up on Wednesday to watch the certification. I make us coffee, and she makes mashed bananas for Juan. I have no jobs today and we are both home cleaning our own house and catching our breath. Olivia wants to go through her parents' things and decide what to give away. I don't know if I can bear it, but I say yes. We turn on Nina Simone, but we've got the news on low in the background and we can see the president telling the crowd the election was stolen.

Sophia and Roberto hated the idea of a president who despised Mexicans and all Latins coming from Central

America. "These aren't people," the president said, "they're animals." Roberto used to repeat that phrase.

"What does it mean when America knowingly elects a man who sees humans like dogs? Who lies all the time?" Roberto would have watched this speech in horror as Trump eggs on his supporters. We stop what we are doing; we turn up the news and turn down the music as the president of the United States tells the mob to go get the vice president and the Congress and make him the president.

"What does he want?" Olivia says. "I don't understand. Are they going to bully Congress into making him president for life like Putin and Xi Jinping and Kim Jong Un? What is the end game here?"

"That's unclear to me too." I say. You can see the crowd is in a full-throated roar; ready for anything. At eleven o'clock our time, they breach the Capitol. One man with horns and a bare chest, several in full military gear, they have zip tie hand cuffs presumably for hand cuffing Congress. We flip from one station to another and finally we see the gallows erected for Pence to be hung on. We hear them crying for Pence who has been whisked away. We see several athletic fellows scaling the walls of the Capitol.

"Stealing the Declaration of Independence is such a big deal in the movies," Olivia says. "Look at these guys. Just walking on in, like they own place. One guy has his feet up on Nancy Pelosi's desk."

We finally feed the baby because that's the next thing to do, but it feels like the country's democracy almost slipped through our fingers just now, today, and if we had a different president, would Sophia and Roberto still be with us today? I feel rage at everyone who voted for Trump.

"What happens next?" Olivia says. "I'm still confused."

"Believe me, so am I. But I think, they'll vote for certification anyhow," I say. I turn down the television and start making the green pozole Sophia used to make. It's late when we gather for soup, tortillas, and beer.

"To the beginning and the end of the world," Olivia says, and we toast.

"To love like your parents had," I say. I want to say, "To forgiveness," but America is so messy. I'm angry on behalf of all of us queer, and poor, and of color, and working hard, all of us out here in the dark, where you don't see us or feel us or know what's happening. You say, I want to help you, but what you mean is, I want to give you a scrap of help so you can keep working for me at that thing you do, whoever you are, you nameless thing, you arms and legs, you feet and hands. But maybe with Trump gone, we will take form, and have our own place inside the house. I'm inside the house now, and I'm burning with desire to make the world right, but I have only my brain and two hands. What country is this that madmen can storm the Capitol and senators can cheer them on?

"Deep thoughts?" Leslie says.

"Rome," I say. "I can't stop thinking about the Roman emperors." Leslie makes each of us a frothy coffee drink and puts in some kahlua. "What else I'm thinking about is the other side of all this. I hope certain wrongs are righted. The Paris Accord. The children in cages at the border. But something bigger. We can't be this people. This is chaos and darkness. That's a Confederate flag celebrating slavery. What are you thinking?"

"I'm thinking that my parents would have been horrified. My dad would have watched all those white guys storming the Capitol and been in disbelief that this is the country he risked his life to come to. It's funny that Americans don't see immigration as a form of flattery. Like come on, people are not trying to immigrate to Russia or China. America should be proud and should try to be its best. That was not America at its best. Do you think we'll get past this?"

"We have to practice kindness. While keeping truth around us." My phone rings and it's Sally.

"Hey," she says. "Chuck wants to talk with you." Chuck comes on.

"I'm sorry for being mean," he says. "It won't happen again. I was wrong. I'm sorry about your friend. She was a really nice person."

"Thank you," I say.

Sally takes the phone. "Rough day," she tells Sally. "But I wanted to call. You be safe." She ends the call.

Olivia shakes her head, "Jesus," she says. "Do we have to start the kindness today?"

Leslie and I put our arms around her, "It's okay, today's a good day for kindness."

"What's your favorite movie?" Leslie says. "Enough politics."

"Movies are just going to remind me of Mama," Olivia says.

"I'll find something," I say.

"You know what I want," she says.

"What is it?" Leslie says. I shake my head.

"Start making the hot chocolate. The thick Mexican hot chocolate."

"Oh, no," Leslie says. "She's going to cry." But she moves into the kitchen with me and gets the chocolate going while I find the movie. I get pillows and blankets so we can all fall asleep in the living room. The baby's monitor is on the table, but who knows, he may sneak out here anyway. Leslie pours out our thick hot chocolate and surrounds each large mug with rose petals from Sophia's garden, and I fire up, *Like Water for Chocolate*, and Olivia, who used to watch this with her mother, begins laughing and crying and we do too, and the country is ours and kindness is all around us, like the taste of chocolate.

THE END

ABOUT THE AUTHOR

KATE GALE IS THE CO-FOUNDER AND managing editor of Red Hen Press, which has been publishing for thirty years in Los Angeles. She is also the author of seven books of poetry including *The Goldilocks Zone* and *The Loneliest Girl*, as well as several librettos including *Rio de Sangre* with Don Davis—who wrote the music to the *Matrix* movies. *Rio de Sangre* premiered at the Florentine opera. Her current opera projects are *Che Guevara* and *Esther.*

Kate grew up in an intentional community. Since leaving, she has put herself through school, ultimately receiving a Ph.D. in English Literature from Claremont Graduate University. She had no one after she left the Farm to depend on, and spent years writing "No one," as her emergency contact. When she briefly met her father, a professor at the University of Pennsylvania, he asked where she was living. She said, "my car," and he asked what kind of car. From those beginnings, she has built a press in Los Angeles, raised a family, and lived a life as a writer and publisher on the West Coast.

Since 1989, she has taught writing at universities in Los Angeles every semester. She has also taught publishing at Oxford, Columbia University, Harvard University, and USC, and was the President of Pen USA from 2005–2006. Currently, Kate teaches publishing and poetry at Chapman University and lives in Los Angeles.

RECENT AND FORTHCOMING BOOKS FROM THREE ROOMS PRESS

FICTION

Lucy Jane Bledsoe
No Stopping Us Now

Rishab Borah
The Door to Inferna

Meagan Brothers
Weird Girl and What's His Name

Christopher Chambers
Scavenger
Standalone

Ebele Chizea
Aquarian Dawn

Ron Dakron
Hello Devilfish!

Robert Duncan
Loudmouth

Michael T. Fournier
Hidden Wheel
Swing State

Kate Gale
Under the Neon Sun

Aaron Hamburger
Nirvana Is Here

William Least Heat-Moon
Celestial Mechanics

Aimee Herman
Everything Grows

Kelly Ann Jacobson
Tink and Wendy
Robin and Her Misfits

Jethro K. Lieberman
Everything Is Jake

Eamon Loingsigh
Light of the Diddicoy
Exile on Bridge Street

John Marshall
The Greenfather

Alvin Orloff
Vulgarian Rhapsody

Micki Janae
Of Blood and Lightning

Aram Saroyan
Still Night in L.A.

Robert Silverberg
The Face of the Waters

Stephen Spotte
Animal Wrongs

Richard Vetere
The Writers Afterlife
Champagne and Cocaine

Jessamyn Violet
Secret Rules to Being a Rockstar

Julia Watts
Quiver
Needlework
Lovesick Blossoms

Gina Yates
Narcissus Nobody

MEMOIR & BIOGRAPHY

Nassrine Azimi and Michel Wasserman
Last Boat to Yokohama: The Life and Legacy of Beate Sirota Gordon

William S. Burroughs & Allen Ginsberg
Don't Hide the Madness:
William S. Burroughs in Conversation with Allen Ginsberg
edited by Steven Taylor

James Carr
BAD: The Autobiography of James Carr

Judy Gumbo
Yippie Girl: Exploits in Protest and Defeating the FBI

Judith Malina
Full Moon Stages: Personal Notes from 50 Years of The Living Theatre

Phil Marcade
Punk Avenue: Inside the New York City Underground, 1972–1982

Jillian Marshall
Japanthem: Counter-Cultural Experiences; Cross-Cultural Remixes

Alvin Orloff
Disasterama! Adventures in the Queer Underground 1977–1997

Nicca Ray
Ray by Ray: A Daughter's Take on the Legend of Nicholas Ray

Stephen Spotte
My Watery Self:
Memoirs of a Marine Scientist

Christina Vo & Nghia M. Vo
My Vietnam, Your Vietnam

PHOTOGRAPHY-MEMOIR

Mike Watt
On & Off Bass

SHORT STORY ANTHOLOGIES

SINGLE AUTHOR

Alien Archives: Stories
by Robert Silverberg

First-Person Singularities: Stories
by Robert Silverberg
with an introduction by John Scalzi

Tales from the Eternal Café: Stories
by Janet Hamill, with an introduction
by Patti Smith

Time and Time Again:
Sixteen Trips in Time
by Robert Silverberg

The Unvarnished Gary Phillips:
A Mondo Pulp Collection
by Gary Phillips

Voyagers:
Twelve Journeys in Space and Time
by Robert Silverberg

MULTI-AUTHOR

Crime + Music: Twenty Stories of Music-Themed Noir
edited by Jim Fusilli

Dark City Lights: New York Stories
edited by Lawrence Block

The Faking of the President: Twenty Stories of White House Noir
edited by Peter Carlaftes

Florida Happens:
Bouchercon 2018 Anthology
edited by Greg Herren

Have a NYC I, II & III:
New York Short Stories;
edited by Peter Carlaftes
& Kat Georges

Songs of My Selfie:
An Anthology of Millennial Stories
edited by Constance Renfrow

The Obama Inheritance:
15 Stories of Conspiracy Noir
edited by Gary Phillips

This Way to the End Times:
Classic and New Stories of the Apocalypse
edited by Robert Silverberg

MIXED MEDIA

John S. Paul
Sign Language: A Painter's Notebook
(photography, poetry and prose)

DADA

Maintenant: A Journal of Contemporary Dada Writing & Art
(annual, since 2008)

HUMOR

Peter Carlaftes
A Year on Facebook

FILM & PLAYS

Israel Horovitz
My Old Lady: Complete Stage Play and Screenplay with an Essay on Adaptation

Peter Carlaftes
Triumph For Rent (3 Plays)
Teatrophy (3 More Plays)

Kat Georges
Three Somebodies:
Plays about Notorious Dissidents

TRANSLATIONS

Thomas Bernhard
On Earth and in Hell
(poems of Thomas Bernhard with English translations by Peter Waugh)

Patrizia Gattaceca
Isula d'Anima / Soul Island

César Vallejo | Gerard Malanga
Malanga Chasing Vallejo

George Wallace
EOS: Abductor of Men
(selected poems in Greek & English)

ESSAYS

Richard Katrovas
Raising Girls in Bohemia:
Meditations of an American Father

Vanessa Baden Kelly
Far Away From Close to Home

Womentality
edited by Erin Wildermuth

POETRY COLLECTIONS

Hala Alyan
Atrium

Peter Carlaftes
DrunkYard Dog
I Fold with the Hand I Was Dealt
Life in the Past Lane

Thomas Fucaloro
It Starts from the Belly and Blooms

Kat Georges
Our Lady of the Hunger
Awe and Other Words Like Wow

Robert Gibbons
Close to the Tree

Israel Horovitz
Heaven and Other Poems

David Lawton
Sharp Blue Stream

Jane LeCroy
Signature Play

Philip Meersman
This Is Belgian Chocolate

Jane Ormerod
Recreational Vehicles on Fire
Welcome to the Museum of Cattle

Lisa Panepinto
On This Borrowed Bike

George Wallace
Poppin' Johnny

Three Rooms Press | New York, NY | Current Catalog: www.threeroomspress.com
Three Rooms Press books are distributed by Publishers Group West: www.pgw.com